Oliver eased the snowy dr___ as he reali___ virtually no traction. It was like driving on an ice rink. And then he saw it. A little red car, lying nose-first in the ditch.

'Damn.' Oliver zipped his jacket up and then walked down the road, his footsteps muffled by the fresh snow.

'Is there anyone in the car?'

He turned in surprise to see Helen standing there, swamped in his bulky jacket, a mobile phone in her hand.

'Get back in the car,' he ordered, glancing at her feet and wondering once again how any woman could walk in such high heels. But he was touched that she cared enough not to even think about herself.

'Don't be ridiculous.' She slithered into the ditch beside him. 'You may be super-doc, but surely even you can't do this on your own. I'm a nurse. I can help.' She reached out and grabbed the torch from him, directing the beam into the car. 'Oh, no! Oliver, there's a baby!'

LAKESIDE MOUNTAIN RESCUE—

romance and drama that will keep you on the edge!

*Siblings Bryony, Tom and Oliver Hunter are
members of the Lakeside Mountain Rescue Team—
they're willing to risk all, ready to save lives!*

*And as winter approaches and
the weather worsens, their skills and their emotions
are about to be tested to the limit…*

*Don't miss these three exciting novels
from Mills & Boon® Medical Romance™ starting with:*

THE DOCTOR'S CHRISTMAS BRIDE…**In
November 2004**: Bryony Hunter has been in love with
A&E consultant Jack Rothwell for most of her life, but
to him she is his best friend. So she decides that the
time has come to date other men. And suddenly Jack
starts to see her in a different light.

This month in THE NURSE'S WEDDING RESCUE
meet GP Oliver Hunter. He is waiting for Miss Right,
but when he finally meets her she's seriously on the
rebound after a disastrous break-up. How is he going
to prove to her that she can love again so soon?

**In January 2005: THE MIDWIFE'S MARRIAGE
PROPOSAL** is Tom's story. Tom Hunter broke up
with Sally Jenner seven years ago, to concentrate on
his career, and now she's back in his life. Despite the
uncontrollable passion between them, she makes it
clear that she isn't going to trust him with her heart
again. But Tom has other ideas...

THE NURSE'S
WEDDING
RESCUE

BY
SARAH MORGAN

MILLS & BOON®

First published in Great Britain 2004
Harlequin Mills & Boon Limited,
Eton House, 18-24 Paradise Road, Richmond, Surrey TW9 1SR

© Sarah Morgan 2004

ISBN 0 263 83939 7

Set in Times Roman 10½ on 12 pt.
03-1204-44340

Printed and bound in Spain
by Litografía Rosés, S.A., Barcelona

CHAPTER ONE

SHE sat on her own at the back of the tiny church, her body unnaturally still, as if the slightest movement might unleash an unstoppable tide of emotion. Her expression was haunted, her eyes fixed forward with the intense concentration of someone struggling for control.

She was beautiful, but it wasn't her beauty that caught his attention.

It was her pallor.

Her cheeks were the colour of the snow that lay thick on the ground outside and even from his prime position at the front of the church he could see the dark circles under her eyes.

She looked like a woman who hadn't slept for days, possibly weeks.

A woman who was holding it together by little more than a thread.

A woman who was about to pass out.

Oliver frowned, his instincts as a doctor battling with his responsibilities as best man. If it weren't for the fact that the bride was due in less than two minutes, he'd have positioned himself next to her because it was his professional opinion that she was about to slide off the pew and collapse onto the stone floor of the little village church.

'Stop ogling the guests.' The man standing at his side jabbed him in the ribs. 'This is my wedding. You're not supposed to be eyeing up the talent. Or,

5

at least, not until afterwards. You're supposed to be supporting me in my hour of stress.'

Oliver dragged his eyes away from the girl and looked at his lifelong friend, a wry expression in his blue eyes. 'Stress? You're finally marrying Bryony, Jack. What's there to be stressed about?'

Jack Rothwell ran a finger along the inside of his collar. 'You should know. You're still single.' He glanced nervously over his shoulder. 'Have you remembered the ring? Are you sure you've remembered the ring?'

'I've remembered the ring.'

'Show me.'

'For crying out loud…' Oliver put a hand in his pocket and then groaned dramatically, his expression horrified as he pretended to fumble for the ring. 'Oh, no! It must be in my other suit!'

'You don't own another suit and you'd better be kidding,' Jack growled, 'or you'll be sorry.'

'Trust me, I'm already sorry,' Oliver said, withdrawing his hands from his pockets and suppressing a yawn. 'This suit is *unbelievably* uncomfortable.'

Jack shot his friend a critical glance. 'That's because it doesn't fit properly.'

Oliver flexed his broad shoulders and grimaced. 'It doesn't seem to allow for muscle.'

Jack's eyes darted nervously to the door. 'Where the hell is your sister?'

'Fashionably late, and watch your language—you're in church,' Oliver muttered reprovingly. 'Stop panicking, will you? She'll be here.'

'And where's your brother? He's supposed to be in charge of getting her here.'

Oliver rolled his eyes and then glanced over his shoulder towards the girl one more time.

She still hadn't moved.

In fact, he had a feeling that if anyone touched her she might crumble. But no one else seemed to be paying her any attention. She appeared to be on her own. In every sense.

She looked so fragile and desolate that something tugged inside him. 'Jack—who is that girl?'

'Which girl?'

'As far as I'm concerned there's only one decent-looking girl in this church,' Oliver drawled, 'but obviously you've lost interest in such things since you proposed to my sister.'

Jack gave a sheepish grin. 'I admit, I'm a hopeless case. Point me to the girl.'

'The one in blue. Sitting at the back. Amazing dark hair.'

Jack looked. 'The one who is about to keel over?'

'That's her.' Oliver's mouth tightened. 'Damn, I hope she's going to be OK.'

'Now you're the one swearing in church,' Jack said mildly. 'That's Helen. One of Bryony's friends from university. The one who's house-sitting for us. Are you sure your sister hasn't changed her mind?'

Oliver wasn't listening. 'So she's the one Bry asked me to keep an eye on,' he murmured softly, his eyes narrowing as they swept Helen's pale face. 'I can see why she was worried. The girl looks as though she's about to collapse.'

'She's had some sort of trauma.' Jack ran a finger around his collar again as another stream of guests flowed into the tiny church. 'Who are all these people?'

'Friends of my family,' Oliver said absently, his eyes still on the girl. 'Do you know what the trauma was? Bryony wouldn't tell me. How crazy is that? She asks me to look after her friend for the next month but doesn't give me any clue as to the problem.'

'That's women for you. Totally illogical.' Jack smothered a yawn. 'But I'm pretty sure it was something to do with a man. Relationships are the pits.'

Oliver raised a dark eyebrow. 'Am I supposed to black your eye at this point? You're standing in church waiting to marry my sister.'

'Well, obviously I don't mean *my* relationship,' Jack amended hastily, glancing towards the door again, 'but think of all the women I had to date before I finally found Bryony.'

'Bryony was under your nose for twenty-two years. It's not her fault you're a bit on the slow side.'

Jack looked at him curiously. 'Did you know I loved her?'

'Of course,' Oliver said wearily. 'Tom and I laid bets as to when you'd finally click.'

'You should have told me.'

'Well, in case you've forgotten, you weren't that keen on the whole concept of commitment,' Oliver said dryly, his eyes flickering back to Helen. 'Is that what happened to her? Did some guy break her heart?'

Jack frowned. 'You're a doctor, for goodness' sake. Hearts don't break.'

'Yes, they do.' Oliver's voice was soft. 'I'm visiting an old lady at the moment who lost her husband of fifty-five years last summer. She's in a mess.'

'That's depression,' Jack said firmly. 'Trust me, her heart is still intact.'

Oliver shook his head. 'Unless I can find her another reason to live, she's going to die. I know it.' He frowned, unable to stop worrying about Hilda Graham, even though technically he wasn't working. 'She's a dear old soul but all her family have moved down south. I need to find her a surrogate family. Someone for her to worry about and care about.'

Jack sighed. 'I just don't get you, Oliver Hunter. You're Mr Rough and Tough on the outside but on the inside you're like marshmallow. I'm amazed you didn't settle down and have fifty children ten years ago.'

'My parents had the perfect marriage. I'm waiting for Miss Right. And when I spot her I'm going to be quicker off the mark than you.' He looked at the girl in the blue suit, thinking that he'd never been so drawn to a woman in his life.

'I'm waiting for Miss Right, too,' Jack muttered, his eyes still on the back of the church. 'And I wish she'd get a move on. At this rate we're going to miss our flight.'

'I still can't believe you're going on honeymoon for a month.' Oliver looked at his friend in disbelief. 'Most people have two weeks, some have three. Four is excessive.'

'Not for what I have planned. We're sorting out Lizzie's Christmas present.' Jack gave a wicked grin. 'Your niece and my soon-to-be stepdaughter wants a baby sister for her Christmas present next year so I figure Bryony and I need to give it our best shot.'

Oliver pulled a face. 'Enough. I don't even want to *think* about you having sex with my sister. And whatever you do, don't say that to Tom. You know how protective he is of Bryony.'

'I'm marrying her, for goodness' sake!'

'I realise that. Why else would I be dressed in this ridiculous outfit?' Oliver glanced down at himself with distaste. 'I honestly can't believe I agreed to this.'

Jack grinned. 'You look beautiful, darling.'

Oliver glowered at him. 'And you're going to look beautiful with matching black eyes.'

'We're in church and your mother is watching us,' Jack reminded him cheerfully. 'You wouldn't dare.'

'Don't bet on it,' Oliver muttered darkly. 'When Ben and Ellie got married they virtually did it in climbing boots. None of this fancy stuff.'

'Your sister wanted a fairy-tale wedding,' Jack said simply, and Oliver shook his head in disbelief.

'Do you know that you've undergone a complete personality change since you put that engagement ring on her finger two weeks ago? You were the guy who was never getting married and here am I dressed like a penguin and pretty soon you're going to have 2.4 children. The world's gone mad.'

'I love your sister. Enough said.' Jack's eyes slid to the girl at the back of the church. 'Helen does look awful, doesn't she?'

'She's going to faint,' Oliver said calmly. 'The only question is, when? Is she ill? She looks ill—rack your brains and try and remember what has happened to her.'

Jack shrugged. 'I wasn't really paying attention. Something about a man and a job.'

'Well, that's helpful!' Oliver shook his head in

frustration. 'You have no interest in your fellow humans.'

'Well, not like you,' Jack admitted. 'That's why you're a GP and I'm an A and E doctor. I heal them and ship them out. Frankly, I don't want to know how they got there and I'm not particularly interested in their lives. You nose around and get involved. You've always been the same—thinking that you can solve everyone's problems. Delusions of grandeur, if you ask me.'

Oliver opened his mouth to retort but at that moment there was a sudden flurry of activity at the back of the church and the organist started to play.

Oliver took a last look at the girl and finally she moved. Her body seemed to tense as the music started and her eyes lifted from the elaborate flower arrangement at the front of the church and locked on his.

Oliver felt something shift inside him.

Suddenly the music faded into the background, along with the sudden buzz of anticipation among the guests. All he was aware of was those huge blue eyes, filled with such naked desperation that he felt his heart twist in sympathy.

It was as if she was begging him to rescue her.

It amazed him that she had the courage to sit there, feeling as bad as she clearly did, and he fought the temptation to stride the wrong way down the aisle, gather her close and keep her safe from whatever it was that was threatening her.

But there was no opportunity.

His sister had already started her walk down the aisle, clutching Tom's arm.

Oliver turned back to the front, vowing to track

Helen down as soon as he could. He just hoped that the girl didn't faint before the ceremony was over.

She never should have come.

Helen clutched her bag tightly, fighting the sickness and the misery, wishing that she'd made an excuse.

But how could she not have come to her best friend's wedding?

Bryony was finally marrying the man she'd been in love with for her whole life.

It would have been selfish of her not to be there for her friend's happiest moment. The fact that it co-incided painfully with her most miserable moment shouldn't signify.

She sat still, reflecting that up until this moment she'd always thought of pain as being something that happened as a result of something physical. She'd nursed patients with broken limbs who'd been in pain, patients with diseases who'd been in pain.

But she was healthy. All the various bits of her body were still attached to each other and functioning perfectly well.

So why did she feel as though she'd been ripped apart?

Her emotions were so dangerously close to the surface that she was afraid that any moment she was going to lose control and allow two weeks of shock and misery to surface in public.

No! She wasn't going to be that pathetic!

If she fell apart then David would have won, and she was not going to let a man do that to her!

Telling herself that she only had to get through the ceremony and then she could hide away, Helen swallowed hard, pressed her nails into her palms and watched as Bryony floated down the aisle, wearing a slinky cream dress trimmed in soft fur. Behind her came Lizzie, Bryony's seven-year-old daughter, dressed in pink and carrying a fluffy purple muff.

Helen's heart twisted painfully and her lips parted in a soft gasp.

It should have been her.

It should have been her walking down the aisle towards a man she loved.

She sat rigid, a lump forming in her throat as she saw Jack turn. His smile was for Bryony alone and everything he felt for her was visible in his eyes as he looked at the woman he loved.

Why did life work out for some people and not for others?

Helen watched, numb, as Jack ignored protocol and scooped an excited Lizzie into his arms, cuddling her close while he exchanged vows with the woman standing at his side.

Suddenly aware that the best man was watching her again, Helen fisted her hands in her lap and made a supreme effort to look casual. She'd never been introduced to him but she assumed that he must be one of Bryony's two brothers.

And she'd already made a total fool of herself by staring at him as though he were a port in a storm. But there was something about his searching, sympathetic gaze that had drawn her to him and she'd found it hard to look away.

She reminded herself that there had to be a reason why he was staring at her and it wasn't likely to be complimentary.

She must look like a hospital case.

Helen almost laughed but at the last moment she

lifted a hand to her mouth, knowing that if she allowed the sound the freedom it craved, it would have been a sob.

Maybe she *was* a hospital case.

She felt so wounded that she couldn't see how she could possibly recover.

Next to her a woman sniffed and rummaged in her bag for a tissue and Helen felt her own tension rise another notch.

No crying.

It was supposed to be OK to cry at weddings, but she didn't dare. She just knew that if she started she would never be able to stop.

And she wished the best man would stop looking at her. Judging from the keen look in his eyes, he'd guessed that something was wrong.

Either that or Bryony had told him.

Helen gritted her teeth, wishing that the ceremony would be over quickly.

She was *not* going to cry.

She was not going to be that pathetic.

'Great speech.' His brother Tom clapped him on the shoulder and Oliver nodded, distracted.

'Yeah—I know. I'm a one-man comedy show. Have you seen the girl in the blue suit?'

She had to be here somewhere.

Oliver peered through the crowd of laughing guests, trying to spot her.

'Why?' Tom lifted an eyebrow quizzically. 'Are you interested?'

Yes. *Very.*

But at the moment he was more worried than interested. He'd somehow missed her in the chaos of photographs at the church and her place had been empty for most of the meal. He needed to satisfy himself that she wasn't lying in a heap on the floor somewhere.

'Oliver, you were a lovely best man.' Bryony approached, her eyes shining with happiness as she stood on tiptoe to kiss him. 'Why are you looking so serious?'

His eyes slid round the room again. 'Bry, your friend, Helen…'

Bryony's smile faded. 'What about her?'

'I saw her in the church. She didn't look good. And now she's vanished.'

Bryony looked worried. 'I honestly didn't expect her to come,' she confessed, glancing around the room with an anxious expression on her face. 'I couldn't believe it when I saw her. I assumed it meant that she was holding up all right.'

'She wasn't holding up all right,' Oliver said flatly. 'She looked a mess.'

'That's why I want you to keep an eye on her for me. She was so devastated by what happened—' Bryony broke off and shook her head. 'I just hate the thought of her being on her own in my cottage.'

'So what happened?'

Bryony bit her lip. 'I can't tell you.'

Oliver's jaw tightened. 'For crying out loud, Bry!'

Bryony sighed, obviously battling with her conscience. 'Well, I don't think she wants people to know. It was one of the reasons she came up here—to get away from the gossip and speculation. I can't tell you details but she's had a bad time. She's wounded—and you're good with everything wounded. When we were children you were always the one who dragged injured animals home. And you usually managed to heal them. You lost your two front teeth fighting with that boy who bullied me at school. Keep an eye on her, Oliver. I don't like the idea of her being on her own.'

'Neither do I.' Oliver's blue eyes glittered slightly. 'And you've let her have your damn cottage, which is in the middle of nowhere.'

'Well, what could I do?' Bryony looked at him helplessly, torn between worry and the desire to defend her decision. 'She had nowhere else to go, Olly.'

Why? Oliver wondered grimly. Why didn't she have anywhere else to go?

'I'll keep an eye on her,' he said finally, leaning forward to kiss his sister's cheek. 'You enjoy your honeymoon.'

Bryony chewed her lip. 'She's lovely, Oliver. Really gentle and kind. She didn't deserve—' She broke off and Oliver gritted his teeth.

'Didn't deserve what? Honestly, Bry, I could strangle you sometimes.'

'Keep your hands off my wife,' Jack said mildly, strolling up and sliding an arm around Bryony's shoulders. 'Is he bullying you?'

'No,' Bryony said softly, ignoring her husband, 'we're talking about Helen. Oliver's going to keep an eye on her.'

'Well, the sooner he starts, the better,' Jack said. 'I saw her vanishing to the ladies' hours ago. Just before your speech. Nearly dived for the toilet myself, in fact—didn't know what you might say.'

'The thing about living in a small community is that everyone already knows all your secrets. It ruins all the surprises.' Oliver grinned and strolled off, leaving the two of them together. There was no sign of Helen anywhere and in the end he gave a little shrug and pushed open the door of the ladies' cloak-room with his usual casual self-assurance.

Perhaps she was still in there.

Helen heard the door to the ladies' open and froze. Then she reminded herself that whoever it was just wanted to renew her make-up and return to the reception as soon as possible.

She sat silent, locked in the privacy of one of the cubicles, waiting to hear the door close again, leaving her in peace.

'Helen?'

The distinctly masculine voice startled her and she stared at the door in horror.

Oh, God, someone had come looking for her!

That was the last thing she wanted. She didn't want to have to face anyone or make small talk.

She didn't want to have to pretend that everything in her life was OK.

'Helen, I know you're in there and if you don't open this door in the next ten seconds I'm going to bust it open so you'd better stand back.'

Helen closed her eyes.

It was the best man. She recognised his voice. The one with the laughing blue eyes and the broad shoulders. The one who'd told a series of anecdotes that had had the entire room in fits of laughter.

'Helen? Please—I know you're hurting but I want you to open this door and talk to me.'

The gentleness in his voice was too much and she felt tears threaten.

No! She wasn't going to cry!

And she certainly didn't want sympathy. Sympathy would be the final straw.

'Please, go away.' Her voice sounded stiff and frozen and for a moment she thought he probably hadn't heard her, then she heard a soft masculine curse.

'Not until you come out.'

'I just want to be on my own.'

'Well, that's tough,' he muttered, rattling the door vigorously, 'because I feel like company.'

She heard a thump and another curse and then the door flew open and crashed against the cubicle wall.

Helen jumped in shock and the best man leaned broad shoulders against the door frame and gave her a smile of smug satisfaction.

'Hi, there. I'm Oliver.'

She looked at the door and back at him, a smile touching her lips despite her misery. 'Not Rambo?'

He grinned and rubbed his shoulder ruefully. 'Fortunately these doors aren't very robust otherwise you'd be giving me a lift to hospital now. It always looks so easy in the movies.'

She breathed in and out slowly, unable to believe that he was standing in the doorway of the cubicle. 'This is the ladies' toilet.'

He didn't shift. 'Then the sooner you come out of there, the less likely I am to be arrested.'

She stared at him bleakly, her face pinched and pale. 'Look, it's sweet of you to bother but I'm fine, honestly…'

'Sure you are.' He smiled a smile that undoubtedly had women falling for him in droves. 'Which is why you chose to lock yourself in the toilet for the entire reception. The food was bad, but not that bad.'

She chewed her lip. 'I can't believe anyone missed me.'

'Well, I did.' His voice was a lazy drawl. 'And I may never forgive you for missing my speech. I was funny. I would have made you laugh.'

Despite her misery, she had to smile. 'You did make me laugh. I heard you from the corridor.'

He nodded and then lifted a hand, sliding it over her cheek and tilting her face towards him. 'He isn't worth it, you know.' His tone was soft and his eyes were speculative. 'Whatever he did to you, you had a lucky escape. And now you can slap my face and tell me to mind my own business.'

His hand was warm and strong and instead of slapping him she felt a strange desire to throw herself on that broad chest and sob her heart out. But then his words registered and her features froze.

'I suppose everyone is gossiping.'

'No.' He shook his head and lifted a hand in a gesture of denial. 'In fact, Bryony refused to tell me anything. But it's pretty obvious to me that it was the wedding that was causing you major problems. My guess is you were planning one of your own.'

She stared at him in disbelief. 'Are you psychic?'

'No.' His tone was gentle. 'I'm a doctor. And I could see that the ceremony was agony for you. Am I right?'

Her eyes filled and she gritted her teeth. 'I really don't want to talk about it.' Her voice was thick with tears and she gave an impatient sigh that was almost a sob. 'I know I'm being pathetic but I can't seem to help it and I'd rather do it in private.'

'You're not being pathetic. On the contrary, I think you're being very brave.'

'Brave?'

She was falling apart in front of him and he thought she was being *brave?*

'Very.' He shrugged. 'Coming to Bryony's wedding when you didn't really want to.'

'I did want to. I love Bryony, it's just that…' Helen fumbled for a tissue and blew her nose. 'Sorry—I'm going to be OK. I just need some time on my own.'

'That's the last thing you need.' He glanced at the door and gave a rueful smile. 'We should get out of here. Sooner or later someone else is going to join us in here and then I think it could get a little bit embarrassing.'

'You go—I'll be fine.'

'I'm not going anywhere without you.'

'I don't want to go out there. I'll bump into someone I know,' she said desperately. 'I don't want anyone asking.'

'I'm a great bodyguard,' he assured her, flexing his muscles in an exaggerated pose. 'If anyone approaches you, I'll knock them down. No questions asked.'

Helen found herself laughing. 'What are you? Mr Good Guy?'

'Dr Good Guy, actually,' Oliver said smoothly, grabbing her hand and dragging her towards the door. 'Come on.'

'I can't go out looking like this.' She gestured to her face, which she knew must look pale and awful. 'I ought to put on some make-up.'

'Why?' He frowned down at her. 'You look beautiful just as you are.'

She stared at him, a lump forming in her throat.

She wasn't beautiful. If she was beautiful David wouldn't have—

'You don't think you're beautiful?' His eyes narrowed speculatively. 'The bastard really did do a good job on you, didn't he? Well, we'll deal with that later but for now we only have two choices. We can go home and I'll make you chicken soup or we can go out there and you can dance with me until your feet are sore.'

'Chicken soup?'

He gave a careless shrug. 'It's my mother's answer to life's problems. You'd be amazed how often it works.'

'Oh.' She rummaged for another tissue and blew her nose. 'You can't go home. You're the best man.'

'Which means you've decided on the dancing.' His mouth curved into a sexy smile. 'Good choice. I'm an amazing dancer. And it gives me an excuse to take this damned jacket off. It's the most uncomfortable thing I've ever worn!'

Helen looked at him helplessly, wondering why he was bothering with her.

'Look, you're being very kind but I really don't think—'

'Good idea—don't think. It's a vastly overrated pastime.' He grabbed her hand and dragged her across the carpeted floor towards the door.

'Wait.' She dug her heels in. 'Please, can you at least let me put some make-up on?'

'No point. You'll only sweat it off on the dance floor.' He pulled open the door just as a group of women approached the toilets. 'Evening, ladies.' He smiled at them warmly, as if exiting from the ladies' toilets was an everyday occurrence for him, and they simply smiled back.

'Hi, Oliver.'

He proceeded to kiss a string of women as they passed and Helen looked at him in amazement.

'Do you kiss *everyone?*'

'If I think I can get away with it.' He let the door swing behind her. 'It's my sister's wedding and this is a small town. We all pretty much know each other.'

Helen digested that. It was such a contrast from London, which always seemed to be full of people leading their own lives in parallel.

'It must be weird,' she said, 'knowing everyone's business and everyone knowing yours.'

Oliver cast her a searching look. 'Actually, it's pretty good,' he said softly. 'Only yesterday I went to see an old man who fell out of bed the night before. The reason I know he fell out of bed was because Pam, who lives next door, happened to notice that he didn't put the bin outside. For the last twenty years he's always put the bin outside on a Friday.'

'And she called you because of that?' Helen looked at him in astonishment and he nodded.

'Yes, but only after she'd let herself in and found him lying there.'

'She had a *key?*'

'Of course.' His shrug suggested that it was normal practice. 'Around here everyone keeps an eye on everyone.'

'That's a nice story,' Helen said quietly, her own problems momentarily forgotten. 'Where I live in London no one has a clue who lives next to them and certainly wouldn't be trusted with a key.'

And then suddenly she realised that she didn't live in London any more.

She didn't really live anywhere.

She didn't have a home. And she didn't have a job.

For a brief moment her heart lurched with panic and then she felt Oliver's hand close over hers, warm and strong.

'And that, my dear Helen,' he drawled cheerfully, 'is precisely why I don't live in London. Welcome to the Lake District, home of snow, rain and neighbours who know what you ate for your dinner!'

Helen laughed and the panic slowly receded. Somehow, with Oliver holding her hand firmly in his, she could pretend that everything was all right. That she'd be able to get through this and come out the other side.

He dragged her straight onto the dance floor, still holding her hand tightly in his. She glanced around her self-consciously but no one seemed to be looking at her.

Which was good, but it still didn't mean she felt like dancing.

Her whole body felt battered and limp. How could she possibly dance?

Surely dancing was an expression of happiness and there wasn't anything good inside her that she wanted to say.

The couples around them were dancing independently to the pounding music, but Oliver slid a warm hand around her back and pulled her firmly against him, forcing her to follow his lead, as if he knew that on her own she was incapable of movement.

'You move your arm, you move your leg...' He

twirled her around, holding her firmly and smiled down at her. 'See? Easy.'

Actually, it felt strange. Being held by Oliver felt strange. Unfamiliar.

She felt the solid muscle of his chest, felt the strength of the arms that held her and breathed in the subtle smell of aftershave mixed with sexy man.

Sexy man?

Helen bit her lip, shocked that she was noticing how sexy Oliver was when she'd been engaged to someone else until two weeks before.

Surely she shouldn't be noticing?

But it was impossible not to notice Oliver Hunter. He was powerfully built, very good-looking and so self-confident that almost every woman in the room was casting wishful glances in his direction.

And he was so different to David. For a start David had been the same height as her and quite slight in build. Oliver was taller and broader and more solid. She knew that Bryony and both her brothers were in the mountain rescue team and she found it easy to imagine Oliver in that role. He was the rugged out-door type, his dark hair cropped short, his hard jaw showing the beginnings of stubble. And he looked totally out of place in formal dress. On his way to the dance floor he'd discarded his jacket and rolled his sleeves up, revealing strong forearms covered in dark hairs. She had the feeling that he'd much rather be in jeans.

He looked tough and capable and very, very male.

'What?' He gave her a lazy smile, his blue eyes trapping hers. 'You're giving me funny looks. Should I be flattered or offended?'

She blushed. 'I've just realised I'm probably hogging the only available male in the room.'

His smile faded and he pulled her closer and swung her in time to the music. 'I'm not available. I'm with you.'

His words made her heart miss a beat and her first thought was one of guilt.

She shouldn't be responding to another man.

And then she remembered that she no longer had any reason not to respond. She could flirt with anyone she liked. *Except that it had been so long since she'd flirted with a man that she'd forgotten how to do it.*

Her cheeks grew pink under his steady gaze. 'You're unbelievably kind.' Her voice sounded croaky and she wondered if he could hear her above the music. 'But I don't want you to spend the evening being kind to me and miss out on the opportunity to meet someone exciting.'

'I've met someone exciting.'

His expression was serious and she gave a little laugh. 'Then you'd better be getting back to her.'

Oliver laughed, too. 'Glad to see that your sense of humour is returning.'

'Returning?' She lifted an eyebrow. 'How do you know I have a sense of humour to return?'

His gaze slid over her face in slow motion. 'Because you have smile lines around your eyes. Dead give-away.'

Helen's smile faded and she felt her tummy tumble. Those compelling eyes locked with hers and tension hummed between them.

Sexual tension. It felt dangerous and deliciously unfamiliar.

As if aware of her thoughts, he stroked a warm

hand down her back. 'Just relax and have fun, Helen. Stop thinking. It's a dangerous pastime.'

She stopped moving, trapped by the expression in his lazy blue eyes and by the feel of his strong hands on her body as he coaxed her closer still.

Close enough to feel the warmth and strength of his body against hers.

Close enough to feel the evidence of his arousal.

Desire curled low in her pelvis and she gave a little gasp and leaned her forehead against his chest, shocked by the power of her own response. *Confused.* Suddenly the dominant emotion she was feeling wasn't pain.

Her fingers tightened on his shirt and she felt the steady thud of his heart through the thin fabric, felt the strength of his body against hers as he held her.

And then she caught a glimpse of Bryony across the dance floor.

The bride.

And reality came rushing back.

She wasn't free to flirt with Oliver Hunter, however sexy he was. She was carrying too much baggage.

'I'm really sorry but I have to go.' She dragged herself out of his arms, cast a last look at Bryony and then fled across the dance floor.

CHAPTER TWO

OLIVER swore fluently and followed her, grabbing his jacket and car keys on the way out of the manor house.

Outside, snow lay thickly on the ground and it was easy enough to spot her footprints forming a pattern that led away from the house.

He gritted his teeth.

Where did she think she was going?

They were in the middle of nowhere and she was wearing ridiculous heels and a thin suit that wasn't designed for winter weather. She was going to freeze to death. And so was he, if he followed her on foot dressed in this ridiculous suit. He glanced down at himself in disbelief, watching as snowflakes settled on his arms, merging with his white shirtsleeves.

Without bothering to put on the jacket, he sprinted to the car park and slid into his car. Switching on the headlights, he drove slowly, squinting into the darkness, until he spotted her halfway down the long drive.

He pulled up next to her and sprang out of the car. 'Are you mad?' He paced in front of her, blocking her path, forcing her to stop. He was still in his shirtsleeves, his bow-tie hanging around his neck. 'It's below freezing out here and you're not even wearing a coat!'

She looked at him blankly, her cheeks pale in the glow of his headlamps. Snowflakes clung to her dark hair and dusted her suit and she was shivering violently. 'I just want to go to the cottage.'

Oliver was about to shout at her for taking such a risk but then he took another look at her and realised that she seemed to be in shock.

And he was rapidly freezing to death.

'You can't walk there,' he said gently, glancing down at her strappy high-heeled shoes with a mixture of disbelief and fascination. If it hadn't been on her foot he wouldn't have known it was a shoe. How did women ever walk anywhere in that sort of foot gear? 'Have you any idea how far it is from here?'

Her teeth were chattering. 'I thought I'd be able to get a taxi from the end of the road.'

Oliver sighed and jerked open the passenger door, guiding her firmly across the slippery drive. 'This is the Lake District, sweetheart, not London. Taxis don't go past the end of the road unless you call them, and even then you usually have to wait for hours while they dig themselves out of a snowdrift.'

She shivered but resisted when he tried to bundle her into the car. 'What are you doing? You can't leave the wedding. You're the best man.'

'And my part is over. Bryony and Jack are leaving to catch their flight soon and the rest of the guests are enjoying themselves.' He gave her a gentle push. 'Get in. I'm taking you home.'

She collapsed into the passenger seat and he closed the door firmly, shaking his head as he saw the marks that her slender heels had made in the snow. It was a wonder she hadn't broken her ankle.

Then he opened the boot and grabbed two thick down jackets from the back seat, vowing that the next time he went to a wedding in early January he was going to wear appropriate dress.

'You might need to rethink your footwear while you're staying here,' he said tactfully as he slid into the car next to her and handed her a jacket. 'Put that on and, please, tell me you have some sensible shoes in your luggage.'

She took the jacket from him, her expression slightly glazed. 'I don't know what's in my luggage. To be honest, I don't know what I stuffed in the case. I dropped it at Bryony's cottage earlier today.'

Oliver eased the car gently down the snowy drive, his teeth gritting as he realised that there was virtually no traction. It was like driving on an ice rink.

'Well, let's hope there's something suitable for tromping around in the snow because we have more than our fair share of it at the moment in this part of the world.'

He pulled onto the main road and cursed slightly as the wheels spun and the car slid away from him. With the ease of experience he turned into the skid, regained control and gently coaxed the car forwards, careful not to touch the brakes.

'Should have brought the four-wheel drive,' he muttered to himself, his large hands strong and steady on the wheel.

'Why didn't you?'

'It's easier to pull when you're driving a flashy car.' He winked at her. 'I thought I might get lucky if I brought the sex machine.'

Helen gave him a wan smile. 'And instead you got stuck with me.'

Her voice faltered slightly and Oliver resisted the temptation to pull over and do something radical to bolster her confidence. The snow was falling thickly and he was afraid that if he stopped the car he might not get it started again.

Assuring himself that he'd be able to concentrate on Helen once he had them both safely home, he flicked on the windscreen wipers, squinting to see through the steady fall of flakes that threatened to obscure his vision.

'If you reach into the back, there's a blanket.' He suddenly realised that, despite his spare coat, she was still shivering. 'Wrap yourself up before you freeze.'

Helen twisted in her seat but before she could do as he'd instructed Oliver caught a flash of red out of the corner of his eye.

Muttering under his breath, he gently brought the car to a halt.

Carefully he reversed a little way back down the road and pulled into a farm gateway. 'Did you see something?'

'No.' Her teeth were chattering now. 'Nothing.'

Convinced that he wasn't imagining things, Oliver flicked on the hazard warning lights and reached into the glove compartment for a torch. 'I'm just going to check. Stay there. I'll keep the engine running and the heater on full.'

He zipped his jacket up and then walked down the road, his footsteps muffled by the fresh snow.

And then he saw it.

A little red car, lying nose first in the ditch.

'Damn.' He sprinted forward and flashed the torch, trying to make out if there were any passengers.

'Is there anyone in the car?'

He turned in surprise to see Helen standing there,

swamped in his bulky jacket, a mobile phone in her hand.

'Get back in the car,' he ordered, glancing at her feet and wondering once again how any woman could walk in such high heels. But he was touched that she cared enough not to even think about herself.

'Don't be ridiculous.' She slithered into the ditch beside him. 'You may be Super-Doc but surely even you can't do this on your own. I'm a nurse. I can help. I've turned your engine off, by the way.' She reached out and grabbed the torch from him, directing the beam into the car. 'Oh, no! Oliver, there's a baby!'

She suddenly seemed galvanised out of her almost catatonic state and Oliver blinked in amazement at the change in her. With some difficulty he transferred his attention back to the car.

'And there's a woman in the driver's seat,' he added grimly. 'Call the rescue services and then get back in my car before you freeze or we'll be rescuing you, too.'

He told her which road they were on and then proceeded to yank the driver's door open. At first it refused to budge, buckled by the force of the accident, but Oliver braced his shoulders and yanked again and this time the door groaned and opened with a hideous cracking sound.

'They're on their way,' Helen muttered, and he realised that she was right beside him again.

'You need to get back in the warm.'

'Don't be ridiculous,' Helen said calmly, ignoring him and reaching into the car to remove the keys. Then she made her way to the boot and opened it.

'What are you doing?' Oliver watched in amazement as she hitched up the skirt of her suit and climbed into the back seat, via the boot, displaying an amazing amount of slender leg in the process.

'I'm checking the baby,' she called back to him, 'while you deal with the driver. And there didn't seem to be any other way in without climbing over your patient.'

Stunned by the change in her and temporarily hypnotised by her fabulous legs, Oliver opened his mouth and then shut it again as he heard the injured woman groan.

In a flash he was beside her, his mind back on the job in hand. 'Hi, there.' His voice was firm and reassuring and then suddenly he recognised the driver. 'Michelle? Oh, you poor thing—what have you been doing? Sweetheart, it's Dr Hunter. You're going to be fine. Can you tell me where you hurt?'

The woman gave a moan and gasped for air. 'Oh, Dr Hunter—thank goodness. What about Lauren? Tell me she's OK.'

'If Lauren is this gorgeous baby, she seems to be fine,' Helen said immediately from her position in the back seat. 'She's still strapped in and doesn't appear to be hurt, but I'm not moving her until the paramedics arrive, just to be on the safe side.'

Michelle gave another gasp. 'The car skidded.'

'The roads are terrible,' Oliver agreed, frowning slightly as he heard her laboured breathing. He flashed his torch to see if he could see visible evidence of injury. 'I need to take a look at you, Michelle, before we get you out of this car. Where are you hurting?'

'Chest…' The woman gave a gulp. 'I can't really breathe properly.' She gave a panicky gasp and Oliver flashed the torch again, this time conducting a swift examination. He shone the light on her trachea and noticed that it wasn't quite central.

Damn.

He heard Helen talking quietly to the baby and then heard the shriek of an ambulance siren and saw the vehicle pull up by the edge of the ditch.

'Michelle, I think you've broken a couple of ribs,' he said gently, 'and one of them has punctured your lung. You've got air where it shouldn't be and at the moment it can't escape. That's why you're having trouble breathing.' And her breathing was becoming more and more laboured by the moment. Grimly aware that he was facing a serious medical emergency, Oliver started to undo the buttons of her coat. 'I'm going to release that air and then you'll be able to breathe again.'

And for that he needed access to her chest.

His gaze flickered to Helen and she gave a brief nod of understanding and wriggled her way out of the boot again, this time minus his coat which was now resting carefully over the little baby.

'Needle thoracotomy. I'll get you a large-bore cannula and some oxygen,' she said quietly, and Oliver watched as she scrambled up the snowy bank, wondering what sort of nurse she was. Obviously a very efficient one. He shook his head as he contemplated how cold she must be in her thin suit.

He turned his attention back to Michelle who was gasping for breath. 'I'm just going to move your coat and your jumper, sweetheart, so that I can get to your lungs. Then I'm going to put a little tube in to drain your lungs and that will make it easier for you to breathe on your way to hospital. You're going to be just fine, angel. Trust me.'

'Here. One 16G IV cannula and oxygen.' Helen handed him the equipment he needed and proceeded to quickly adjust Michelle's clothing so that he had access to the side of her chest. 'We can't undress her in this weather so I'll just hold her clothes while you do it.'

Oliver glanced at her. 'The paramedics lent you a jacket.'

'That's right. Just a shame they don't have the same size feet as me,' she said ruefully, and Oliver laughed.

'Michelle, I wish you could see this woman's shoes.' As he spoke he was swabbing the skin and getting ready to insert the cannula. 'You've never seen anything more ridiculous in your life. Just a few pieces of ribbon and a heel that looks like a lethal weapon.'

Michelle gave a weak smile as she breathed through the oxygen mask. 'I love shoes, Dr Hunter,' she rasped, and Oliver rolled his eyes.

'Women! You're incomprehensible.' He used his fingers to find the right position and then gave Helen a quick nod to warn her that he was about to perform the thoracotomy. 'All right, Michelle. This might be a bit uncomfortable for a second but it's really going to help you breathe, sweetheart. Hold Helen's hand for a minute. It will help warm her up. Heaven knows, she needs all the help she can get.'

Somehow Helen managed to hold the patient's clothes out of the way, angle the torch so that he could see what he was doing and provide the necessary comfort and reassurance.

'How are you doing, Oliver?' One of the paramedics stuck his head through the other side of the car and Oliver gave him a nod.

'Steve, can you get Lauren out and into the warm while I finish up here?' he requested, his expression grim. 'And then we'll need a backboard to be on the safe side. I know about the ribs and the lung but I haven't had a chance to assess the rest of her.'

Because she was going to die if he didn't act soon.

As he spoke, Oliver unsheathed the cannula and used his other hand to feel for the second intercostal space. He would have preferred anaesthetic and sterile conditions but unfortunately neither was available. 'This will hurt a bit, Michelle,' he warned, but she barely flinched as he pushed the needle in. Instantly there was a hiss of gas and Helen released a breath herself.

'Bingo.'

'Give me some light on her face.'

Helen flashed the torch again and Oliver was relieved to see that Michelle's colour had improved immediately and that her breathing was already easier.

'That's quite a party trick,' Helen muttered. 'I thought you were a GP.'

'And that makes me brain-dead?' Oliver glanced at her quizzically. 'Am I supposed to be offended?'

'No.' She laughed and looked a little embarrassed. 'But none of the GPs who I worked for in London would have been able to do what you just did, I'll tell you that now. Have you done A and E?'

'In my youth,' Oliver said, carefully checking Michelle's breathing. 'But I deal with emergencies all the time in the mountain rescue team.'

Despite the steadily falling snow, she was still right

beside him, this time holding a roll of tape in her hand. 'Better secure that cannula,' she advised, tearing off some tape and handing it to him. 'Don't want to undo that good work. Inserting chest drains in freezing weather in the dark isn't to be repeated, however impressive it seemed the first time.'

He hid his surprise. Less than an hour ago the woman had been in a sodden heap of misery at his sister's wedding. Now she was brisk and professional, standing right beside him as they dealt with the accident, seemingly oblivious to her high heels and the fact that the weather was bitingly cold.

It was distraction therapy at its most bizarre.

'Do you want to put a tube in here?'

Oliver adjusted the oxygen mask over Michelle's mouth and nose, his hands steady and reassuring.

'No. It's too cold. I want to ship her and the baby out as fast as possible, Steve—' He glanced over his shoulder at the paramedic, who was hovering. 'You can be in the hospital in ten minutes if you don't skid off the road.'

Steve grinned. 'I'll let that one pass because I know you're baiting me.'

'Would I?' Oliver adjusted his position. 'I'm just going to check her over and then we'll get her out.'

Ten minutes later Michelle was safely in the ambulance.

Steve looked at Oliver. 'Are you coming?'

Oliver hesitated. He really had no choice. Michelle's condition could deteriorate again on the journey. On the other hand, it would mean taking Helen too because there was no way he was leaving her by the side of the road.

Before he could answer they saw headlights approaching and a car slowed down as it approached them.

'What's going on?' Ben MacAllister, one of the A and E consultants who had been at the wedding, wound down his window. 'I'm on my way to work because they just rang me in desperation. Just dropped off Ellie and the baby. Looks like they're getting another customer. Do you need help?'

Oliver nodded and quickly told him what had happened. 'You could go in the ambulance just in case she needs attention. I should get Helen home. She's not exactly dressed for the hills and I don't want to have to treat her for hypothermia.'

Ben parked his car next to Oliver's and climbed into the ambulance without discussion.

Satisfied that his part in the drama had ended, Oliver grabbed Helen by the wrist and guided her across the slippery road and back to the car.

CHAPTER THREE

THE cottage was down a narrow country lane but Helen was shivering so violently that she barely noticed where they were going. Now that the emergency was over, she suddenly realised that she was desperately cold.

Oliver pulled up outside the cottage and bundled her inside, flicking on lights as he went and kicking the front door shut behind him.

'Upstairs, straight away.' His expression grim, he hurried her up the staircase into a warm, cosy bathroom. 'Strip.'

Helen stared at him, her teeth chattering. 'Pardon?'

He sighed and raked a hand through his soaked hair. 'Sorry—that didn't come out quite the way I intended it to. You're soaking wet, sweetheart, and we need to get you warmed up. Get in the shower.'

Helen was shivering so violently she couldn't make her fingers move. 'You go downstairs first.'

'No way. This is no time for modesty.' Oliver took a step towards her, strong hands reaching forward and stripping off the jacket that the paramedic had lent her. 'I'm not leaving you until I'm sure you're OK.'

'I'm OK,' Helen protested weakly, wondering if she'd ever feel warm again.

'You will be once you're in that shower and I've made you a hot drink.' He dropped the jacket on the bathroom floor and frowned. 'You're totally soaked through.'

He removed her suit jacket and then started to unbutton her blouse but she covered his hands with hers.

'Stop it! I can't undress with you here.'

Oliver muttered something under his breath. 'I'm a doctor, for goodness' sake.'

He might be a doctor but he was also a man. Six feet two of broad-shouldered, attractive man. There was no way she could undress in front of him.

'I'll be fine,' she muttered, but he ignored her and unzipped her skirt and removed her blouse in a deft movement.

Left standing only in her underwear, she gave a gasp of embarrassment and protest.

'Close your eyes!'

'Oh, for goodness' sake.' He glanced at her impatiently. 'How many naked women do you think I've seen in my time?'

'Millions probably.' She shivered. 'But you've never seen me.'

Muttering under his breath, he tugged the clip out of her damp hair and pushed her towards the shower. 'Move.' His tone was wry. 'I never seduce frozen women. Believe it or not, I prefer them thawed.'

Left with little choice, she stepped into the shower and closed her eyes with a gasp as the hot water sluiced over her frozen skin, the warmth delicious after the bitter cold of the snow and ice.

'Oh, that's bliss.' She kept her eyes closed as the feeling gradually returned to her toes and her legs and her numb hands.

When she finally opened her eyes and scraped her soaked hair away from her face, the first thing she saw was Oliver standing there, holding a huge fluffy towel.

'Dry yourself off and then get dressed. I've put some clothes on the radiator to warm.'

She switched off the shower and grabbed the towel. 'What about you? You're wet, too.'

He gave a wry smile. 'My jacket was waterproof and I wasn't virtually barefoot. Let's sort you out first.'

She wrapped the towel around herself and stepped out of the shower cubicle but the shivering immediately started again.

'Damn.' Oliver cursed softly and dragged her against him, rubbing her skin with the towel until she gasped.

Then he reached and grabbed some clothes from the towel rail, thrusting them into her arms. 'Here we are. Take off your wet underwear and get dressed in these. They're Bryony's so they should fit. Wear them until you have a chance to sort your own stuff out. There's a hair-dryer on the landing. I'll go and make a hot drink.'

Oliver boiled some milk and reviewed his options.

He'd been expecting to go home after the reception, but he didn't want to leave Helen in this isolated cottage on her own.

The adrenaline rush of dealing with the emergency may have driven her out of her depressed state, but he had little doubt that the recovery was only temporary and there was no way he was leaving her to fester.

He grabbed two mugs from Bryony's cupboard and located the hot chocolate.

Tomorrow was Sunday and technically he wasn't

working, although he did plan to make a few impromptu visits on patients who were worrying him.

Like Hilda.

'Hi, there.' Helen stepped up behind him, her cheeks flushed from the warmth of the shower, her dark hair falling soft and loose around her shoulders.

Oliver felt his gut clench as he looked at her.

Without the ridiculous heels she barely reached his shoulder, and now that she was wearing a pair of his sister's thermal pyjamas and a fluffy dressing-gown she looked younger and more vulnerable than ever. Seeing her in proper light for the first time, he detected dark smudges under her blue eyes and lines of tiredness that suggested that she hadn't slept properly for weeks.

He gritted his teeth and resisted the temptation to pull her into his arms.

'Here…' Instead, he handed her a hot-water bottle and pulled out one of the kitchen chairs. 'Sit there and warm up while I finish making us both a drink.'

She sat without argument and Oliver spooned chocolate powder into the mugs and added the milk.

'So you knew that woman in the car? Michelle?' She cuddled the bottle close and hooked her feet around the legs of the chair. 'Is she one of your patients?'

Oliver settled himself opposite her and handed her a mug of chocolate. 'Yes. I look after the whole family. Her baby, her brother and both her parents. Tom delivered Lauren.'

Helen slipped her hands around the mug. 'Bryony has told me about Tom. He's a consultant obstetrician, isn't he?' She took a tentative sip and smiled at him gratefully. 'This is delicious.'

'Didn't you meet Tom at the wedding?'

Helen stared into her mug, her smile fading. 'I didn't meet anyone at the wedding. I spent most of the time avoiding people,' she confessed and then nibbled her lip. 'I was probably horribly rude.'

Oliver cursed himself for bringing up the subject of the wedding. 'You weren't rude, Helen,' he said gruffly, 'you were upset.'

She was silent for a moment and then she put her mug down on the table and looked at him. 'You must be wondering what I'm making all this fuss about.' Her blue eyes were huge in her pale face. 'Bryony didn't tell you, did she?'

'Bryony is a very loyal friend,' Oliver said immediately, 'and you don't have to tell me anything you don't want to. Only if you think it might help.'

'Nothing is going to help.' She gave a wan smile. 'Except maybe extreme violence.'

He laughed, remembering how gentle she'd been with the baby. How she'd ignored the freezing temperatures in order to keep the little scrap warm.

'You don't strike me as a violent person.'

She looked at him, her expression serious. 'Actually, I felt violent,' she confessed, a slight shake in her voice. 'For the first time in my life I really felt like being violent. Isn't that awful?'

'No.' Oliver frowned slightly. 'I expect you had provocation.'

'I think so.' She took a deep breath. 'My fiancé called me from the airport to say that he was on his way to Singapore and that he wouldn't be able to make our wedding after all.' Her tone was light but she was gripping the mug so tightly that her knuckles were white. 'We were due to go to Singapore together after the wedding, you see, first as our honeymoon and then as part of his new promotion. I gave up my job and he rented out his house where I just happened to be living, too.'

Oliver saw the pain and panic in her eyes and suddenly felt pretty violent himself. 'Well, he's obviously a bloody idiot,' he said calmly, pushing her mug towards her. 'Finish it. It will warm you up.'

'That's not all.' She took the mug but she didn't lift it to her lips. 'He took a girl with him. Some young hotshot lawyer he'd been working with. He said that he'd suddenly realised that things weren't going to work out between us. And then he hung up.' She shook her head as if she was still trying to make sense of it. 'That was it. I didn't even get the chance to see him in person.' She looked at him blankly. 'There was so much I wanted to ask him. I wanted to know how long he'd felt like that. It couldn't have been a sudden thing and yet he chose to wait until the day before our wedding.' She lifted a hand and rubbed her forehead. 'I should have spotted something.'

'Stop blaming yourself for his deficiencies.' Oliver lounged back in his chair and let out a long breath. 'No wonder you found Bry's wedding difficult.'

She gave a wan smile. 'Technically I shouldn't even have been there. I should have been on my own honeymoon.'

Oliver winced slightly, hardly able to imagine how difficult it must have been for her. 'So that's why Bry lent you the cottage.'

'I didn't have anywhere else to go,' she said simply, finally finishing her chocolate and toying with the mug. 'I no longer have a home or a job. When I called

Bryony she immediately said that I should come up here, and I have to confess that I jumped at the chance, even though it's the coward's way out. I couldn't bear the thought of seeing all my colleagues in London or facing my relatives.'

Oliver saw the traces of colour leave her pretty face as she contemplated her situation.

'Well, this is a pretty good place to recover,' he said softly, reaching across the table and removing the mug from her fingers. She was gripping it so hard he was afraid she might shatter the china. 'It will work out, Helen. Trust me.'

She gave him a brave, lopsided smile. 'Is that your professional judgement, Dr Hunter?'

'Absolutely.' His eyes gleamed. 'And first thing to-morrow I'm going to sort out your recovery pro-gramme. But for now you need sleep.'

'I'm not that great at sleep.'

'You will be tonight,' he assured her. 'Mountain air does it for everyone. Go on up, you look shattered. You're in the bedroom at the front.'

She frowned at him, clearly puzzled. 'What do you mean, I'm in the bedroom at the front?'

'I'll take the spare room,' Oliver said calmly, com-ing to an instant decision. There was no way he was leaving her. He decided that she needed distraction. 'Or I can sleep with you in yours if you prefer.'

Just as he'd planned, the colour flooded back into her cheeks and she gave a shocked gasp. 'Is that an-other professional suggestion?'

'Absolutely not.' Oliver gave her a sexy wink. 'It was an extremely *unprofessional* suggestion.'

She gave a hesitant laugh, but her blue eyes were suddenly wary. 'You're staying here? Seriously?'

'Didn't Bry tell you?' Oliver's expression was innocent and he reassured himself that the slight deception was more than justified by the circumstances. 'I'm having some work done on my house and I needed somewhere to live.'

'Oh…' She looked startled. 'What work?'

'I…er…roof,' Oliver said, and then kicked himself. Only an idiot would have their roof done in the middle of a freezing January. He tensed, waiting for her to see through his feeble excuse, but Helen didn't seem at all suspicious and he reminded himself that she was used to London. When did they last see real snow in London? She probably couldn't begin to imagine what a Lake District winter could be like. He exhaled slowly. 'So, actually, I'll probably be here for most of January, too.'

'What—living here?' She frowned slightly and he rose to his feet and scooped up both mugs.

'Sure.' He turned his back on her and kept his tone casual. 'What's wrong with that? I won't get in your way.' *Well, not much.* 'And I don't suppose you'll get in mine.'

He stacked the mugs in the dishwasher, pressed the rinse button and turned to face her, his expression neutral.

'Right.' Her smile faltered slightly, as if she wasn't quite sure how she should be reacting. 'I'm not sure which bedroom is Bryony's…'

'I'll show you.'

He took her upstairs and pushed open a door. 'This is it. You should be comfy in here. You know where the bathroom is. My room is across the landing and this…' he flung open another door '…is Lizzie's room. On second thoughts, maybe I'll sleep in here.'

He studied the room thoughtfully and Helen burst into laughter.

'You wouldn't fit in the bed and somehow I can't see you sleeping surrounded by pink.'

'Pink has always been my favourite colour,' Oliver said solemnly, and she leaned against the wall, still laughing.

'Don't tell me—you can't get to sleep without a bedroom full of stuffed toys.'

Oliver decided that he'd endure any amount of pink and stuffed toys if it meant that he could see Helen laugh. For a brief moment her eyes sparkled, a sweet dimple appeared in her cheek and she looked so adorable that he caught his breath, pierced by a sudden need to kiss that soft mouth.

Desire shot through him and he struggled to keep it under control, reminding himself that this woman was seriously on the rebound.

Not a good prospect whichever way you looked at it.

'Oliver?' Her smile faltered. 'You're looking at me oddly.'

'Sorry.' He made a monumental effort to pull himself together. 'Well, I hope you sleep well. Goodnight.'

'Goodnight.' Her reply was soft. 'And thank you for everything tonight.'

He frowned slightly. 'I didn't do anything.'

'You got me through the second most difficult day of my life,' she said simply, and then stepped forward and kissed him on the cheek. 'And I'm very grateful.'

And with that she melted away into Bryony's bedroom, leaving Oliver suffering from a severe attack of lust.

*　　*　　*

Helen was woken by the delicious smell of fresh coffee and the sound of male voices in the kitchen.

Struggling to shake off the remains of a deep sleep, she glanced at the clock by the bed and realised to her surprise that it was already nine o'clock.

How could she possibly have slept so late?

For the last two weeks she hadn't been able to sleep at all. So why, last night, had she managed to sleep right the way through? Maybe Oliver was right about Lake District air.

She lay there for a moment, warm and snug under the soft duvet, a shaft of light peeping through the curtains as she hovered between sleep and wakefulness.

Male laughter intruded on her doze and she woke fully and sat up.

Since David had called her from the airport, getting out of bed had proved to be the biggest challenge of every day, but today, for some reason that she couldn't identify, it didn't seem so bad.

She dressed quickly and wandered downstairs, curious as to who Oliver was talking to.

Pushing open the kitchen door, she saw him sitting with his feet on the table, chatting to his brother, Tom.

'Good morning…' Feeling suddenly shy and wondering if she was interrupting something, Helen started to back away but Oliver was on his feet in an instant, treating her to that easy, sexy smile that seemed to be his specialty.

'Sit down and I'll pour you some coffee. This is Tom.'

'Hi, there.' Tom gave her a friendly nod and Helen slid into a chair, feeling very self-conscious. Fortu-

nately both brothers dived straight back into their conversation about a rescue that had obviously taken
place the week before and, realising that neither of
them was taking much notice of her, Helen relaxed
and just listened.

Although Tom was a similar build to Oliver and
had the same dark hair and blue eyes, he seemed to
have a completely different personality. While Oliver
was relaxed and friendly, Tom seemed reserved and
cool, his handsome face giving away little as he
talked.

'We're a dog team down until Ellie's willing to
leave the baby,' he was saying, and Oliver nodded,
his gaze flickering to Helen.

'In bad weather a dog can search much more ef-
fectively than a human,' he explained, leaning over
and handing her a steaming mug of coffee. 'Ellie, one
of our staff nurses, is a member of SARDA—that's
the Search and Rescue Dog Association, but she had
a baby a few weeks ago so she's out of action for the
time being.'

Helen listened as they chatted about other members
of SARDA they'd worked with.

Finally Tom yawned and glanced at his watch. 'I'd
better make a move. I'm popping into the hospital.
I've got a couple of ladies ready to pod that I'm not
entirely sure about.' He glanced at his brother. 'Are
you going to be at home later?'

'I might call in,' Oliver said casually, his eyes fixed
intently on his brother's face, as if he was trying to
communicate something, 'but of course I'm staying
here for most of this month because of the work I'm
having done on my, er, roof.'

There was a long silence while Tom looked at his brother and then he stirred. 'Your roof.'

'That's right. My roof.' Oliver smiled. 'I'm just lucky Bry's away so that I can stay here while it's happening.'

Tom picked up his coat. 'Amazing planning on your part.' He smiled at Helen. 'See you around. Walk me to the car, Oliver, I need to give you that ice axe.'

'All right, what the hell is going on?' Tom folded his arms across his chest and glanced back at the house. 'You've moved in here?'

'Keep your voice down.' Oliver frowned at him and Tom gave a suggestive smile.

'Well, that's fast, bro, even for you. But, then, she is extremely pretty.'

The fact that his brother found Helen pretty bothered Oliver more than he could possibly have imagined, and he gritted his teeth and consoled himself with the fact that he and Tom never fell for the same type of woman.

'You saw her at the wedding. She was a mess. I didn't want to leave her on her own.'

'Right. So this is, of course, a completely altruistic gesture on your part.' Tom's voice was loaded with irony. 'And what's all this rubbish about your roof?'

Oliver raked long fingers through his cropped hair. 'I needed an excuse to not live in my house. I told her I was having my roof done.'

Tom threw his head back and laughed aloud. 'In the middle of January while it's snowing? And she believed you?'

'She's a southerner. They don't have proper winters in the south,' Oliver said, glancing towards the house to make sure that Helen wasn't listening. 'I was caught on the hop—I didn't know what else to say. I just knew that I couldn't leave her on her own and don't think she has much experience of fixing roofs.'

'For your sake, I hope you're right,' Tom said, waggling his finger at his brother, 'or you are in big trouble. So exactly what form did this comfort take last night? Horizontal?'

Oliver glared. 'Don't be disgusting.'

'Ah…' Tom's eyes glittered with speculation. 'My little brother has come over all protective. So I take it you didn't sleep with her?'

Oliver gritted his teeth. 'I did not. She's been through a bad time.'

'So what she needs is another man to take her mind off the rat who broke her heart,' Tom drawled, unlocking his car and throwing his jacket inside. 'Simple. If you don't think that's you, let me know. I'm sure I could cheer her up.'

Oliver's hands curled into fists. 'Lay one finger on Helen and I'll knock you out cold,' he said icily, and Tom straightened up, the smile fading from his handsome face.

'Whoa.' His voice was soft, all the mockery gone as he put a hand on his brother's shoulder. 'Are you serious about her?'

Oliver sucked in a breath and suddenly realised that he was. 'Crazy isn't it? I've only known her for five minutes.'

Tom's grip tightened momentarily. 'Well, that's all it takes for some people.' He frowned and let his hand drop. 'Be careful, Oliver. If she's been that badly hurt she could be bad news for you.'

'I'll take my chances. To be honest, the biggest problem at the moment is getting her through the next few days. The only time she seemed to function properly was at the accident last night.'

'Accident?'

Oliver related what had happened and Tom shrugged. 'Well, she had something to take her mind off her problems. Sleep with her and it will have the same effect.'

Oliver looked at his brother in naked exasperation, conveniently forgetting the direction his thoughts had taken the night before. 'Do you ever think about anything but sex?'

'Not really.' Tom yawned. 'I'm an obstetrician. I'm confronted by the by-product of sex on a daily basis.'

But Oliver wasn't listening. 'What I need is to find her a job,' he muttered, an idea forming in his mind. 'She's a practice nurse.'

'You've already got a perfectly good practice nurse. You don't have enough work for another one.'

'That's true.' Oliver's expression was thoughtful and Tom gave a sigh.

'What's on your mind?'

'I've got a plan.'

Tom rolled his eyes. 'I thought you might have. And no doubt it involves giving the lovely Helen a job. What are you going to do? Fire Maggie?'

Oliver shook his head. 'No need. I've thought of a much better solution.'

'I daren't even ask,' Tom said wearily, and Oliver looked at him.

'What about you?' He forced himself to ask the question. 'Are you interested in her—seriously?' He held his breath, waiting for his brother to answer, but Tom gave a slow shake of his head.

'No. She's very pretty, but...' He shrugged dismissively and it was Oliver's turn to frown.

'You do realise that you haven't been serious about a woman since Sally, don't you?'

'You sound like one of those daytime chat show hosts.' Tom's eyes were suddenly shuttered, his face blank of expression. 'I'm serious about my career. That's enough.'

Oliver suddenly realised that although they were as close as brothers could be, Tom never, ever talked about Sally. He talked about women and dating and sex, but never about Sally Jenner, despite the fact he'd never been seriously involved with a woman since. Surely after seven years he should be able to talk about her? Unless she still meant something to him. Unless he was regretting the split...

Knowing that he was on dangerous ground, Oliver sucked in a breath. 'Tom...'

'This is a pretty serious conversation to be having outside Bry's cottage on a snowy Sunday morning, don't you think?' Tom drawled lazily, turning back to the car and sliding into the driver's seat. 'If you're still feeling like analysing the meaning of life this evening, you can meet me at the Drunken Fox and we'll get seriously hammered. In the meantime, I've got lives to save.'

He slammed the door, hit the accelerator and roared off at a speed that made Oliver wince.

Making a mental note to force a proper conversation about Sally at some point, Oliver reached into his pocket and grabbed his mobile phone.

His call to Maggie, his practice nurse, yielded the

result he was hoping for and he strode back inside the cottage feeling thoroughly satisfied with the way his morning was going.

Pushing open the kitchen door, he was hit by the delicious smell of sizzling bacon. While he'd been outside with Tom, Helen had cooked bacon, made fresh coffee and cut some slices of bread from a loaf.

'I thought you might like breakfast,' she said, and he stared at the plate on the table.

'There's only one plate.'

She flushed. 'I'm not hungry.'

Oliver smiled placidly and settled himself at the table. 'I'll only eat if you eat, too, sweetheart.'

She chewed her lip and lifted the bacon from the pan onto the plate. 'I don't—'

'Helen.' His tone was patient. 'You didn't eat a thing yesterday and you need some energy for what's happening today.'

Her eyes flew to his. 'What's happening today?'

'I need to make some calls and I need you to come with me.'

'Me?' She looked surprised, as well she might. 'Why me?'

Because he had things to do and he had no intention of leaving her sitting brooding in the cottage.

'You were very good at that accident last night,' he said casually, cutting two more slices of bread and putting them on her plate. 'You're obviously a fabulous nurse and once you've eaten something I have a proposition to make.'

She sank into a chair opposite him. 'A proposition?'

'Yes.' Oliver forked bacon onto the bread and pushed the plate towards her. 'Eat.'

'But…'

He smiled placidly and took a huge bite out of his own sandwich. 'Eat.'

She did as she was told, although her bite was more of a nibble. 'What's your proposition?'

'I need a practice nurse.'

She put the sandwich down on her plate. 'I'm not looking for a job, Oliver, I don't think I can.'

'Let me finish.' He smiled at her, wishing that he could do something to bring colour to her cheeks. Even after a decent night's sleep, she still looked pale and tired. 'It would just be temporary. Our practice nurse has gone to Australia for a month to see her new granddaughter. We're pretty desperate.'

Helen frowned. 'But surely if you knew she was going…'

'It was a sudden decision on her part,' Oliver said glibly, consoling himself with the fact that it *had* been a sudden decision, so he wasn't exactly lying. 'It would be impossible to find someone just for a month.'

'You want me to work in your practice for a month?'

'It would be great if you could,' Oliver said fervently, realising that if she said no he was in serious trouble. He'd just given his delighted practice nurse a month's leave and there was no way he could withdraw the offer. If Helen refused to step in, his partners would lynch him.

'I—I don't know,' she stammered, lifting her coffee mug and then putting it down again without taking a sip. 'I hadn't even thought about work, to be honest.'

'Well, what are you going to do all day if you don't work?'

'I don't know.' She stared at her hands as if she hadn't actually given the subject any thought until that moment. 'I thought I might read a few books, go for walks...'

Oliver remembered her footwear and resolved to check the way she was dressed before she went for a walk. The mountain rescue team spent an inordinate amount of time rescuing people who'd ventured into the hills in unsuitable foot gear.

'I'll take you for walks,' he promised. 'I'll show you the area. When we're not working.'

She coloured slightly. 'But—'

'I'll do you a deal.' His gaze was steady on hers. 'You help me out of my crisis and work in my practice and I'll show you the Lake District. I guarantee that by the time I finish you won't want to set foot in grimy, traffic-clogged London again.'

She smiled and he could tell she was wavering. 'I don't know anything about working in a rural practice.'

Oliver shrugged. 'It's exactly the same as working in any other practice. People still get sick with the same things and have the same problems as they do in London. Our practice nurse runs an asthma clinic once a week and does the immunisations with the health visitors. All the usual sorts of things. And if you have any worries you can always come to me.'

'What about your partners?' She bit her lip. 'Wouldn't they want to interview me or something?'

Oliver shook his head. 'I have two partners—Ally Nicholson, she's the wife of Sean, one of the A and E consultants. They were both at the wedding. And then there's Hugh Bannister. He's great, too. Once I tell them how brilliant you are, Ally and Hugh would just be grateful to you for helping out.'

She sat silent for a moment and he could see that she was weighing up the pros and cons.

'I haven't brought a uniform with me.'

'I'll call Ellie,' Oliver said immediately. 'You two must be about the same size and she won't be using hers for a few months. It will be fine.'

Helen looked at him, clearly unsure what to say now that final excuse had been dealt with.

'All right,' she said finally, 'if you're sure you want me.'

Oh, he definitely wanted her. In his practice and in his bed, preferably every day for the rest of his life.

Reminding himself that he had to take it one step at a time, Oliver pushed her sandwich towards her.

'Great. When you've finished breakfast, get some warm clothes on. There are some patients I want to see.'

CHAPTER FOUR

SHE still couldn't quite believe that she'd agreed to this.

She'd fled to the Lake District expecting to spend a month licking her wounds alone in Bryony's little cottage.

But so far, apart from her long sleep, she hadn't had five minutes alone.

And now she was going to be working in a full-time job and Oliver was living in the cottage with her so there was absolutely no way she was going to be able to find the privacy to brood.

Oh, well, maybe that was a good thing, Helen thought as she climbed into the four-wheel drive next to Oliver. After all, brooding wasn't going to change anything. Brooding wasn't going to bring David back.

She glanced across at Oliver, suddenly very conscious of his hard, powerful brand of masculinity. If she had to find one word to describe him, it would be 'strong.' Everything about Oliver was strong. He was the sort of man who could handle anything. The sort of man that everyone would turn to in a crisis.

Including her.

And if he'd been eye-catching in the formality of a dinner jacket, he was even more handsome in casual clothes.

A pair of ancient jeans clung to the solid muscle of his thighs and a thick jacket emphasised the breadth of his shoulders.

Suddenly wondering why she was noticing the way Oliver looked, Helen fumbled with her seat-belt. It was just because he was such a dependable person, she told herself. And she was feeling vulnerable.

'Are you OK?' He smiled at her. 'Boots OK?''

Helen glanced down at her feet, now encased in a pair of sturdy boots. 'They're great. Surprisingly stylish.'

Oliver grinned. 'Believe it or not, even Bryony refuses to totally sacrifice style for practicality. Those are her everyday boots. When I take you walking you'll need something more sturdy. And you'll need to borrow some extra layers.'

'I'm already wearing hundreds of layers.' Helen fingered the waterproof jacket, still feeling vaguely uncomfortable at having borrowed her friend's clothes.

'I hope Bryony doesn't mind about this.'

'Well, she's not wearing them,' Oliver said logically, glancing over his shoulder as he turned the vehicle in the drive, 'and you're about the same size, fortunately.'

'I could have managed with my own clothes.'

'Helen—' his tone was patient '—your case was full of London clothes. Great for parties and lunches but we don't do a lot of that up here. Here you're more likely to be rescuing a stray sheep from the side of the road and that's easier if you're not in stilettos.'

She couldn't resist teasing him. 'And you've tried it in stilettos, of course.'

His glance was solemn. 'I ruined my favourite pair doing just that.'

She laughed, amazed by how comfortable she felt

with him considering she'd known him for less than twenty-four hours.

He pulled out onto the road and switched on some music, his hands firm and confident on the wheel. 'So did you do a lot of that in London? Parties and lunches?'

'My fiancé—ex-fiancé,' she corrected herself swiftly, 'is a lawyer and he expected me to do lots of entertaining.'

He glanced at her curiously before returning his attention to the road. 'I can't imagine you enjoying all that. Did you?'

Suddenly realising that she'd never even asked herself that question before, Helen was silent for a moment. 'No,' she said finally, 'I don't think I did particularly. It was a lot of pressure and they were nearly always strangers and I was expected to behave in a certain way…' She glanced down at herself again and gave a small smile. 'If David could see me now, he'd throw a fit.'

Oliver winked at her. 'Then maybe we should send him a photo,' he drawled, and she laughed.

'He'd hate me dressed like this, that's for sure. His idea of casual dress is something tartan with a label.'

'Oh, trust me, you're wearing serious labels.' Oliver smiled. 'But they're mountain labels. That gear will gain you instant credibility up here. Everyone will immediately assume that you know how to fasten your crampons.'

Helen looked at him in alarm. 'Then perhaps you'd better tell me what they are.'

Oliver laughed. 'Metal teeth that you fasten to the bottom of your boots when you want to walk on snow or ice.'

Helen looked at him doubtfully. 'Why would I want to walk on snow or ice? It sounds dangerous.'

'It's fun.' Oliver flicked the indicator and turned down a side road, pulling up outside a row of cottages. Then he turned to face her, something glittering in his blue eyes as he looked at her. 'If David would hate you dressed like that then the man is obviously a fool.'

Taken aback by the compliment and the look in his eyes, Helen caught her breath. 'I know you're just trying to make me feel better,' she muttered, 'but thank you anyway.'

'I'm not trying to make you feel better,' Oliver said calmly, undoing his seat-belt and reaching into the back for his coat. 'I think you're the most beautiful woman I've ever seen, apart from the black circles under your eyes—but we'll get rid of those soon.'

The most beautiful woman he'd ever seen?

Helen glanced at him, startled, and then looked away quickly, thoroughly flustered by the warm appraisal in those wicked blue eyes.

'So who are we seeing here?'

'My Hilda,' he said evenly. 'I don't know what to do with her. I'm waiting for inspiration so any suggestions will be gratefully received.'

'What's her problem?'

'She lost her husband last summer and "lost" is the operative word.' He reached into the back of the vehicle for his bag. 'She no longer has a reason to live.'

'That's awful.' Helen felt her heart twist with sympathy. 'It makes me feel very selfish and self-indulgent, stewing in my own worries.'

Oliver turned to her with a frown and his hand

covered hers. 'No, don't think that. You're entitled to feel sad and cheated. But you'll recover because David obviously wasn't the right man for you, and once you realise that you'll be fine.' He let go of her hand and jumped out of the car. 'Unfortunately, that isn't the case for Hilda. Barry was wonderful and she adored him. Can you imagine that? Being with the same person for fifty-five years?'

He shook his head and started to walk up the path towards the cottage. Helen followed him, still thinking about what he'd said.

David wasn't the right man for you.

Of course David was the right man. Helen frowned, suddenly feeling confused. She'd loved him. Really loved him. She'd agreed to marry him, for goodness' sake.

But she didn't have time to dwell on Oliver's words because the door to one of the cottages opened suddenly and a woman stood there, her silver-grey hair and her slightly bent posture betraying her age.

'Dr Hunter.' She gave a tired smile and shook her head. 'Don't you have anything better to do than bother me on a Sunday?'

'I'm afraid not.' Oliver spread his hands apologetically. 'There's no food in my house, I'm starving hungry and I thought you might have made one of your amazing chocolate cakes.'

Hilda gave a sigh and looked at Helen. 'He pretends that I'm doing him a favour when, in fact, we both know that he's just checking up on me.'

'This is Helen. She's my new practice nurse,' Oliver said, gently nudging Hilda back inside the house and gesturing to Helen to follow her inside.

'She's helping me out until Maggie gets back from Australia.'

Hilda looked startled. 'But I saw Maggie yesterday and she didn't say—'

'She managed to get a flight last night,' Oliver interrupted smoothly, 'so finally she's going to see that new granddaughter of hers. It was all very much a last-minute thing.'

'Goodness, it must have been.' Hilda looked startled and then smiled and took them into the small living room. 'Well, that's excellent news,' she said wistfully, and then turned to Helen. 'My family are all down south and it's too far for them to come, although they're very good about phoning. I lost my Barry last year, you see.'

'Dr Hunter told me,' Helen said gently. 'I'm so very sorry.'

'Well, we knew it was coming.' Hilda gave a wan smile. 'He was very ill but thanks to Dr Hunter he didn't suffer. He's an amazing doctor and I owe him so much.' She glanced at Oliver who was looking decidedly uncomfortable. 'I suppose you're too busy for a cup of tea.'

'I'm never too busy for a cup of tea,' Oliver said immediately, and Helen hid her surprise.

In the London practice where she'd worked, she'd never known the doctors accept a cup of tea. In fact, it was pretty rare that they did their own house calls, she reflected. They nearly always handed them over to a deputising service.

But not only was Oliver saying yes to tea, he'd actually wandered through to the kitchen to put the kettle on himself.

'The cake is in the tin, Dr Hunter. You know which

shelf,' Hilda called after him, turning back to Helen with a sad smile. 'Poor Oliver.' Her voice was soft. 'He so badly needs to fix everything for everyone. He was the same as a child. Always wanting to put things right. But not everything in this life can be fixed.'

'He's worried about you.'

'I know. He's a dear boy.' Hilda sighed and flexed her fingers, looking down at her wedding ring. 'And he shouldn't keep coming here. There are plenty of sick people out there who need him and there's nothing wrong with me. I'm just lonely.'

'Do you go out at all, Hilda?'

'Well, the bus service isn't that great from here,' the older woman confessed, 'and most of the time I just don't have the energy. And now there's snow on the ground I'm afraid of slipping and breaking something.'

Helen nodded, glancing up as Oliver strolled in carrying a tray loaded with tea and an enormous chocolate cake.

Hilda looked at the cake. 'Did you bring a knife to cut that, dear?'

'No need for a knife,' Oliver said smugly. 'I can eat it as it is.'

Hilda laughed. 'You're just like my Barry. He never could resist my chocolate cake either. What about you, Helen, will you have a slice?'

She'd barely eaten for a fortnight and suddenly, in the space of a few hours, she'd been confronted with a bacon sandwich and now chocolate cake. Helen opened her mouth to refuse politely and then caught Oliver's eye.

'I'd love some,' she heard herself saying weakly. 'It's my favourite and it does look really delicious.'

It *was* delicious, and for someone who didn't think she had an appetite, Helen devoured her slice with remarkable ease.

They spent another hour with Hilda, and Oliver talked openly about things that were happening in the surrounding villages, things that he thought might interest Hilda.

Her face lit up as she joined in the conversation, talking about people she'd known since she was a girl. But when they finally rose to leave there was no missing the desolation in her eyes and Helen found it hard to tear herself away.

'I don't like leaving her there on her own,' she confessed, and Oliver sighed wearily.

'I know. It really gets to you, doesn't it?'

'Would she move house? She seemed quite animated when you talked about things that were happening. This is a pretty lonely spot. Perhaps if she was in the centre of town she wouldn't feel so isolated.' Helen frowned, remembering what Hilda had said about being afraid to go on the bus in the winter.

'She and Barry lived in that house for the whole of their marriage.'

'But she doesn't have Barry anymore,' Helen said softly. 'She needs company. She needs to get involved in the community.'

Oliver gave her a thoughtful look. 'To be honest, it never even occurred to me to suggest that she think about moving. She's lived in that cottage since she married Barry so I assumed that she wouldn't want to leave it.'

'But her life has changed.' Helen brushed a strand of dark hair behind her ear. And perhaps she can't build a new life if she's still surrounded by the old one.'

She frowned, realising that she could be easily talking about herself, and Oliver's blue eyes gleamed with understanding.

'So you think my Hilda should throw out her stiletto heels?'

Helen smiled. 'Something like that.'

'Well, it's certainly a thought.'

'At least you know about her and you're keeping an eye on her.' Helen gave a wry smile. 'I have to confess that in London, I don't think anyone would have checked on her unless she'd called the surgery.'

'Hilda has never called the surgery,' Oliver said dryly, unlocking his car and dumping his bag inside. 'Hilda would rather die quietly than bother anyone. She'd just become steadily more and more depressed.'

But that wasn't going to happen while Oliver was around.

As Oliver fastened his seat-belt his hand brushed hers and Helen looked at him, suddenly noticing the thickness of his dark lashes and the creases around his eyes.

He was gorgeous.

Confused by her own thoughts, she looked away quickly, her heart thudding steadily in her chest.

Two weeks ago she'd assumed that she was going to be spending the rest of her life with David. How could she so quickly find another man attractive?

She'd never been the sort of girl to flit from one romance to another.

David had been her first proper boyfriend.

Quickly she turned her attention back to Hilda. 'I suppose it's important to just keep watching her.'

'Oh, I'm watching her,' Oliver said calmly. 'It's very easy to dismiss depression in the elderly. You say to yourself, "Well, she's old and lonely, what do you expect?" whereas, in fact, a proportion of elderly patients will have a clinical depression that can be helped by medication.'

'But you haven't prescribed anything for her yet?'

Oliver shook his head. 'And I don't want to unless I'm sure she needs it. But I will if I have to.'

Helen nodded. 'If you like, I could do some digging around to see if there are any suitable properties.'

Oliver shot her a curious look. 'You don't know the area.'

'If I'm seriously going to be working here then I'd better hire myself a car,' Helen said practically, 'in which case I'll have the means to get out and explore.'

Oliver was silent for a moment. 'No need to hire a car,' he said finally, starting the engine and releasing the handbrake. 'You can drive this one. I'll drive my sex machine.'

Helen laughed. 'But how will you get any work done with all those women throwing themselves at you?'

'It's a killer,' he admitted ruefully, 'but I'll work it out somehow. I'm sure if I concentrate I can fit them into my busy schedule.'

Helen shook her head, still laughing. She loved his sense of humour. 'It's kind of you, but you've already done too much. I can't steal your car as well.'

He shrugged. 'Macho though I am, even I can't drive two cars at the same time.'

'But, Oliver—'

'Just say yes.'

'But—'

'Do all townies argue as much as you?' he growled, checking in his rearview mirror before pulling out. 'Just say yes.'

She smiled. 'Yes. Are all country guys as much of a bully as you are?'

'We know how to treat our women.' He grinned wickedly and it occurred to her that this man most certainly didn't need a flashy car to pull women. He just had to smile.

'So where are we going next?'

'Into town. I want to check on a baby.' He pulled onto the main road and drove towards town. 'She had a febrile convulsion on Thursday. The mother was pretty shocked by it all.'

'I'm not surprised. Did you admit the child?'

He nodded. 'First febrile convulsion, so yes. We always admit any child under two who has a febrile fit, those with serious infections and those where we can't find a cause for the fever. Otherwise, after the first one, we teach the parents to give rectal diazepam so that they can manage it themselves if the child has further febrile fits.'

He parked in the street and switched off the engine.

'It says "No parking."' Helen peered up at the sign doubtfully, but Oliver just smiled as he pulled his bag from the back seat.

'That's for tourists, sweetheart.'

As if to prove his point, at that moment a female

traffic warden wandered down the street and gave them a cheerful nod.

'Good morning, Dr Hunter.'

'Morning, Tracey,' Oliver returned, locking his car. 'How's that ankle doing?'

'Much better since I did those exercises.' She looked at his car. 'I'll keep my eye on that for you, Dr Hunter. We've had some problems along this road in the last few months. Just kids, I suppose, but, still, you can't be too careful.'

'Thanks, Tracey. We're just popping in to see little Pippa Dawson.'

The traffic warden tutted sympathetically. 'I heard that the poor mite was in hospital. Give them my love.'

She gave them a cheery wave and walked on down the street, leaving Helen staring after her open-mouthed.

'She's a *traffic warden?*' She shook her head in disbelief. 'In London they have horns and tails. Scary.'

'Oh, Tracey can be scary.' Oliver laughed as they crossed the road and walked along the snowy pavement. 'You should see her in the summer. The cars are festooned with tickets.'

'So why do you deserve special treatment, Dr Hunter?'

He winked at her. 'That would be telling.' He paused outside a small terraced house and rang the bell. 'This shouldn't take long.'

But Helen noticed that he didn't seem at all resentful to be seeing patients at a weekend. The GPs she'd worked with in London had all grumbled on the rare occasions they'd been on call on a Sunday, but Oliver seemed to be thoroughly enjoying himself.

'Hello there, Lauren.' He greeted the young mother with his usual smile. 'Just popped in to see how little Pippa is.'

'Oh, Dr Hunter, I wasn't expecting you to call.' Visibly flustered, Lauren tried to smooth her hair. 'The house isn't very tidy.'

'I haven't come to make an offer on your house, Lauren,' Oliver said gently, 'and if you think your house is in a mess, you should come and look at mine. And I don't have a sick baby to use as an excuse.'

Lauren relaxed and gave him a wide smile. 'Well, it would be great if you could look at her. We were up all night with her again. She's a lot better, of course, but she's still not right.'

'You poor thing—you must be totally knackered. This is Helen, by the way.' Oliver waved a hand to indicate Helen as they walked into the house. 'She's acting as my practice nurse while Maggie has a well-earned break.'

'Oh, have you finally persuaded her that you can survive without her for five minutes?' Lauren led them into a tiny sitting room. 'Pippa's in here. I put her in her bouncy chair for a change of scene. She was crying so much I didn't know what to do with her.'

'Did the hospital give you a letter for me?'

Lauren nodded and lifted a brown envelope from the top of the television. 'They did all sorts of tests but in the end they just said it must be a virus.'

Oliver smiled sympathetically. 'Irritating isn't it? We train for all these years just to say it's a virus that we can't identify. But those tests will have excluded some worrying infections, Lauren, so in a way that's good news.' He put his bag down and strolled over to the baby who was kicking her legs in her chair.

'I left her in just a vest and nappy because of her temperature,' Lauren said anxiously. 'I'm so terrified she might have another one of those fits. It was awful. I keep worrying about it in case it means she's an epileptic.'

'It doesn't mean that, Lauren,' Oliver said firmly. 'Very young children can't control their temperatures the way you and I can, and that's why they fit. Only a minute percentage go on to develop epilepsy in later life, and although there are no guarantees I'm sure Pippa isn't going to be one of those.'

Lauren bit her lip and shifted a pile of laundry from the sofa. 'But she might be.'

'Well, let's put it like this.' Oliver tilted his head to one side, his expression thoughtful. 'If you buy a lottery ticket tomorrow and I tell you that you have a one in a hundred chance of winning, are you going to go out on a mad spending spree before you hear the numbers?'

Lauren laughed. 'No, of course not. If the odds were one in a hundred then I know for sure that it wouldn't be me.'

'Well, those are the odds,' Oliver said firmly, 'so let's treat it like the lottery, shall we? It's so unlikely to happen that there is no point in planning for it. Now, can I take a look at her?'

Considerably reassured, Lauren bent down and undid the straps that held the baby in the seat while Oliver scanned the letter from the hospital.

'It looks as though they were pretty thorough. Now, then.' He tucked the letter into the pocket of his jeans and dropped to his haunches in front of the baby. 'Hello, sweetheart, you're looking a lot better than you did when Uncle Oliver last saw you.'

Smiling and pulling faces at the baby, he slid large hands around her tiny body and gently lifted her up.

Helen watched, transfixed, intrigued by how comfortable Oliver was with the baby.

'She's so gorgeous, Lauren,' he murmured, holding the baby against his shoulder, running a hand over the downy head, feeling her fontanelle. 'She doesn't feel so hot now. When did she last have Calpol?'

'Not since last night,' Lauren said. 'Her temperature seems to go up in the evenings.'

Oliver nodded. 'That often happens. I'm just going to lay her on the sofa so that I can examine her.'

Helen watched while he worked, noticing how skilled and gentle he was with the baby.

'Stop smiling at me, madam,' he murmured as he undid her nappy. 'It's no good. You are so gorgeous I'm going to have to take you home with me.'

'Well, you're welcome to her at night,' Lauren said dryly. 'I'd give anything for an undisturbed night.'

'What about your mum?' Oliver finished his examination and redid the nappy deftly. 'Can't she have her for a night? I know you're still breast-feeding but you could always express. Do you good to have a night off.'

'I just can't get her to take a bottle.' Lauren gave a helpless shrug. 'I know she's using me as a comforter but it's easier to let her do that than have a screaming battle.'

Oliver pulled a face. 'It's a tough one. Who's your health visitor?'

'Jenny Stevens.'

'Give her a ring,' Oliver suggested, lifting Pippa confidently and giving the little girl a last cuddle. 'Jenny has all sorts of tricks up her sleeve. She might be able to suggest something.'

'I don't want to be a bother.'

Oliver handed the baby back to her. 'You're not a bother, Lauren. You're a tired mum. I think Pippa's on the mend but if you're at all worried you can take her straight back to the hospital. Or you can call me. You've got my mobile number.'

'Stuck by my phone,' Lauren confessed ruefully. 'Thanks, Dr Hunter.'

They walked back to the car and Helen looked at him in amazement. 'You gave her your mobile phone number?'

'That's right.' Oliver slung his bag in the car. 'It saves her having to call several numbers before getting through to me. It's scary seeing your own baby fit. I didn't want her to feel she was alone.'

'None of the doctors I worked for would have given out their phone number,' Helen muttered, and he lifted an eyebrow, clearly puzzled.

'Why not?'

'They would have been too afraid that someone might use it,' Helen said dryly, and he laughed.

'I would have thought that was the general idea, but I'm willing to believe that it's different in London. I suppose, to be honest, I wouldn't give it to any patient I wasn't sure of, but they're pretty good around here and I've known most of them for years.'

She looked at him curiously. 'Did you always want to be a GP?'

'Always. And so did Bryony. We used to play doctors' surgeries when we were little.'

'Not doctors and nurses?'

'Doctor and doctor.' Oliver glanced sideways and gave her a sexy wink. 'But any time you want to play doctors and nurses, let me know. I'm a quick learner and it definitely sounds like my sort of game.'

Helen laughed. He was so open it was impossible to be offended. 'You're going to get yourself in trouble one day, Dr Hunter.'

'Oh, I do seriously hope so.' He chuckled and she rolled her eyes and changed the subject hurriedly.

The more she saw of Oliver Hunter, the more she liked him.

And she was starting to like him a lot.

'Where now?'

'Back home for some lunch and then to the mountain rescue base to check on some new equipment that was due to arrive yesterday.' He drove steadily, his eyes fixed on the road ahead. 'Then we'll create something amazing in the kitchen for our dinner.'

'But you're on call.'

'No I'm not. Time off for good behaviour.' He flashed her a smile. 'Ally is on call this weekend.'

Helen stared at him. 'But you've been seeing patients.'

'Not really. I just saw Hilda because I was worried about her, and I wanted to check up on Pippa because I knew Lauren would be worrying herself sick about her. They weren't emergencies and I certainly wouldn't expect either of my partners to make those calls. Now I'm going back to the Sunday papers.'

He cared enough to check on patients on his day off.

And now he felt he had to entertain her.

'You could just drop me back at the cottage,' she

suggested, 'and then you could do whatever it is you usually do on a Sunday.'

'I'm doing what I usually do on a Sunday,' he said easily, 'only this time I have company.'

'I can't imagine you're short of company,' she said, with a wry smile in his direction. Women probably flattened each other in the race to get to him. Why he was wasting time with her was beyond her comprehension. Or maybe it wasn't.

Oliver Hunter obviously had a thing about anything injured or hurting, and at the moment she came under that heading.

She didn't kid herself that he was being anything other than kind.

She was just someone that he had to heal, like his patients.

They were just pulling up outside the cottage when his mobile phone rang. He switched off the engine and answered it.

Even with her limited experience, it was obvious to Helen that someone was in trouble on the mountains.

'I'll be there in ten minutes,' Oliver said tersely, and snapped the phone shut, starting the engine again immediately. He turned to Helen with a frown. 'I'm really sorry, I'm going to have to leave you—someone has been reported overdue. They should have returned from their walk by now but there's no sign of them and the mountain rescue team has been called out.'

'Don't worry about me.' Helen jumped down from the vehicle, conscious that she was slowing him down.

But he didn't immediately drive away. His hard jaw was tense and his eyes searched hers.

'I don't like leaving you.'

She was unbelievably touched. 'Oliver, I'll be fine. I don't need watching. I'll have a quiet afternoon.'

His mouth tightened. 'I don't want you to have a quiet afternoon. You'll brood.'

'I won't brood.' She gave a lopsided smile. 'I'm not that pathetic. I'll make something for our dinner.'

Oliver sighed, visibly torn, and then he muttered something under his breath and raked long fingers through his cropped hair. 'All right, although I've no idea what time I'll be home. Don't wait up for me. Call me if you need to. My mobile number is stuck on Bry's notice-board in the kitchen.'

Oliver didn't arrive home until nine o'clock and by then Helen was chewing her nails and staring out of the window, looking for his headlights.

When he finally walked through the door she flew to meet him. 'I was so worried about you…'

Oliver unzipped his jacket and gave her a curious look. 'That's nice.' His voice was soft. 'No one usually worries about me, apart from my mother.' His eyes settled on hers for a long moment and she flushed, wondering what the matter was with her. She'd known him for less than twenty-four hours and here she was, acting like a clingy wife.

But she'd been scared that something had happened to him—

'Sorry, I—I just thought you'd be back hours ago,' she muttered, suddenly embarrassed, and he stepped towards her and took her face in his hands.

'Don't apologise,' he said gruffly, his thumbs stroking her cheeks. 'It's nice that someone missed me.'

His gaze was warm and assessing and suddenly Helen felt seriously flustered. He dominated the narrow hallway of Bryony's cottage, his shoulders almost filling the space. His jaw was dark with stubble, his cropped hair was damp from the snow and there was no escaping the fact that he was incredibly good-looking.

For a moment he stared down at her and she had a breathless feeling that he was going to kiss her.

'Your hands are freezing.'

He gave a rueful smile and his hands dropped. 'Sorry. It's pretty cold out there.'

'I made you some soup,' Helen said quickly, dragging her gaze away from his and hurrying through to the kitchen. Of course he wouldn't have kissed her. She was imagining things. Why on earth would he kiss her? 'You might not be hungry, but—'

'I'm starving,' he said dryly, hanging up his jacket and following her. 'Believe me, tramping around the fells for nine hours works up an appetite.'

She heated the soup slowly and Oliver sprawled in one of the kitchen chairs and closed his eyes with a groan.

'I'm knackered.'

She shot him a sympathetic look. 'Did you find them?'

His eyes opened and he yawned. 'Eventually. But they weren't where they said they were so that caused some problems.'

'Why were they walking in this weather? There's snow on the ground.' Helen stirred the soup slowly and Oliver laughed.

'Because the snow makes the landscape beautiful, my little city girl. Plenty of people 'round here like to walk and enjoy the hills at this time of year.'

Helen smiled ruefully and poured the soup into a large earthenware bowl. 'I'm sorry. I must seem like an alien to you. I was born in London, I went to university in London and I've worked there ever since.'

Oliver gave a dramatic shudder. 'It's a wonder you're even remotely sane,' he teased, sniffing appreciatively as she placed the bowl on the scrubbed pine table in front of him. 'At least they taught you to cook in London. Smells delicious.'

Helen cut two large slices of bread and Oliver looked at her in surprise. 'That looks home-made.'

'It is.' Helen gave a shrug. 'Not much else to do here in the country when it's snowing outside. I had to find a way of amusing myself and Bryony's cupboards are very well stocked.'

Oliver gave a slow, sensual smile that made her insides tumble. 'We country folk have all sorts of exciting ways of passing the time when the weather is bad.' He picked up the spoon, his eyes twinkling wickedly. 'If you're good, I'll teach you a few.'

Her tummy did a somersault.

He was flirting with her again and she didn't know how to handle it.

Unsettled by her reaction to his good-natured teasing and feeling totally flustered, Helen flicked on the kettle and generally busied herself around the kitchen.

'So do lots of people go walking in the fells in the middle of January?' She couldn't imagine the appeal and she found it hard to understand that some people would choose to be out in that weather.

'Plenty.' Oliver tore the bread with his fingers. 'And if they're well equipped, that's no problem. Unfortunately the group today didn't have what they needed to survive in this weather. Snow changes things. You can't see the paths. Landmarks look different. It's easy to get lost.'

'But you didn't get lost.' She couldn't imagine Oliver Hunter lost in any situation. He was the sort who others would depend on. Someone who would always lead.

'We have satellite navigation equipment, which helps us pinpoint our exact position.' He looked at her hopefully. 'Is there any more soup?'

Pleased that he was enjoying it so much, she poured the remainder into his bowl. 'But presumably you didn't always have that technology.'

'Before satellite navigation we used compasses and good old-fashioned local knowledge.' Oliver helped himself to more bread. 'And, believe me, you can't beat old-fashioned knowledge. Most of us were brought up in these hills. When Tom and I were kids we used to play a game. We'd identify a fixed point, usually miles away, and then we'd walk to it, memorising landmarks on the way. Then we'd return by the same route, using the landmarks to stop ourselves getting lost.'

Helen looked at him blankly. 'What sort of landmarks?'

Oliver shrugged. 'A rocky outcrop in a funny shape. A huge boulder with a stream running nearby. Sometimes it was just a patch of sheep dung.'

'And did you ever get it wrong?'

Oliver grinned. 'Never. We had far too much pride to get lost. And by the time we were teenagers we knew the local area so well that we could have walked it with our eyes shut. It was good training for mountain rescue. I'm intimate with an enormous number of boulders between here and Keswick.'

Helen shook her head. 'It's so different from my childhood.'

'Tell me about your childhood.'

Helen settled herself in the chair opposite him. 'It will sound very boring to you, I'm sure.' She frowned slightly. 'My dad was a lawyer in a London firm. I went to a girls' day school. Mum stayed at home and managed Dad's life.'

'No brothers or sisters?'

'No.' Helen gave a lopsided smile. 'I would have loved a sister, actually.'

Oliver nodded. 'I always imagine that it must be pretty hard to be an only child. All that weight of parental expectation on your head.'

Helen nodded, thinking of her parents' ambitions for her. 'And the trouble is when you disappoint them there's no one else to take the attention away from you.'

'I can't imagine you ever being a disappointment.'

Helen sighed. 'My parents really wanted me to marry David,' she said simply. 'They were totally crushed when it all fell through. Embarrassed, humiliated, angry.' She rubbed her forehead with shaking fingers, suddenly realising that the sanctuary she'd found was only temporary. At some point she was going to have to face people again. 'Their reaction was one of the reasons I escaped up here. I could have stayed at home, but they were both so distraught by what had happened that it made the whole situation even more stressful.'

Oliver looked at her keenly. 'You're talking as if the whole thing was your fault.'

And that was part of the problem, of course. She'd gone over it a million times in her head.

'Well, I must have had something to do with it.'

'For crying out loud, he was the one who rang you from the airport!' Oliver's tone was incredulous. 'He was a total coward. The only good thing about the way he behaved was that it surely showed you that you had a narrow escape.'

'Escape?' Helen looked at him. Up until now she'd just been trying to cope with the shock. Trying to adjust to the fact that her future was no longer the way she'd planned it.

Oliver sighed. 'Would you really want to marry a man who would treat you like that?'

Helen bit her lip. 'I don't suppose it's his fault if he had second thoughts.'

'It's his fault that he didn't stand his ground and face you. He was totally cowardly and he didn't think about your feelings at all. Just himself.'

It was true, of course. David had only been thinking about himself.

'What would you have done?'

'If I'd changed my mind about getting married?' Oliver let out a long breath. 'Well, that's hard to say because I wouldn't make a mistake like that, but if I did then I would definitely have told you face to face.'

Of course he would.

Only a coward would do it the way David had and Oliver Hunter was certainly no coward.

This man wouldn't run from anything.

'My mother thought he was the perfect man.'

Oliver's mouth tightened. 'So why didn't she marry him instead of you?'

Helen smiled. Sometimes she had been a little exasperated, seeing her mother fawn over David.

'She had my best interests at heart. I suppose she worried about me. Her idea of a perfect life was to find a rich man and marry him. She gave up work as soon as she met my dad. She basically ran Dad's life. She wanted the same for me.'

'What about her own life?'

Helen frowned. 'Well, Dad was her life.'

'And that's what you wanted for yourself?' It was Oliver's turn to frown. 'Would you have given up work?'

Helen was silent for a moment. 'David wanted me to, but I loved my job. To be honest, we'd reached the point where we couldn't discuss it. It made him angry. My mother was hoping that once the fuss of the wedding was over, I'd come to my senses and resign.'

'You're a brilliant nurse, Helen. Why would you want to give it up?'

'Sitting here with you, I don't want to give it up,' she confessed, 'but back in London, surrounded by people giving me advice, it isn't quite so easy.'

'Then we need to make sure you don't go back to London.'

She laughed. 'What, you mean hide here with you forever?'

'Now, there's a thought.'

Her smile faded. For some ridiculous reason that she couldn't begin to understand, the prospect of hiding here with Oliver filled her with excitement and warmth.

Telling herself that it was just because he was providing a convenient bolthole, she turned the subject back to him. 'Didn't your parents worry about you? Didn't they have expectations?'

'My dad was a climber,' Oliver told her. 'He trained as a doctor, but all he ever wanted to do was climb. He was always disappearing for weeks at a time to try out a new route on some rock or other. He said that climbing was the most fun that anyone could have, and he encouraged the three of us to climb the moment we could walk.'

'And your mum didn't mind?' Helen looked at him curiously. It was so different from her own background that she found it hard to even imagine what it must have been like to be a child in the Hunter household.

'Mum loved Dad for who he was, and climbing was part of who he was,' Oliver said simply. 'Of the three of us, Tom was probably most like Dad. Bryony and I were happy to mess around on the fells here. Tom wanted the big stuff. He and Dad climbed together in the Alps and the Himalayas.'

'Didn't your mum worry?'

'I'm sure she worried herself sick.' Oliver gave a wry smile. 'But she would never have stopped any of us doing what we wanted to do. It was always our decision. She probably worried more about Tom than me. I think she had a few pangs when he went to the Himalayas.'

Helen winced. 'I'm sure she did.'

'Mum was very good at letting us follow our own paths,' Oliver said thoughtfully. 'I think she realised that if she tried to stop Tom, he'd do it anyway and then there'd be a rift between them. So she just made sure that he had the very best equipment and that he climbed with people he could trust. At one point we all thought Tom would spend his life climbing. Then suddenly he announced he wanted to be a doctor and that was that. He put the same energy into that as he had into his climbing.'

'He seems young to be a consultant,' Helen observed, and Oliver grinned.

'Don't tell him that. He's arrogant enough as it is. Much as it pains me to admit it, my brother is a bit of a hotshot.'

His pride in his brother was obvious and Helen thought again what a thoroughly nice man he was.

'So, Miss Helen Forrester.' Oliver stood up and lifted his plate and bowl from the table. 'That's my life history.'

'Sit down. I'll clear up.' Helen tried to take the dirty plates from him but he hung onto them firmly.

'You cooked it,' he reminded her, and Helen bit her lip.

'But you've been out all day, and—'

'So?' Oliver's tone was questioning. 'Why does that mean you should be the one to clear up?'

She flushed slightly. 'You've had a hard day, and—'

A muscle flickered in his hard jaw. 'Is that what he used to say to justify sitting on his backside while you ran 'round after him?'

The directness of his question caught her by surprise. 'Yes. No. I mean, his job was much busier than mine and—'

'Helen.' Oliver interrupted her and this time there was no trace of amusement in his voice. 'Don't make excuses for him. And for your information, I don't expect you to clear up after me. While we're living together we share the load.'

Gently but firmly he removed the plates from her fingers and put them in the dishwasher. Then he turned and pushed her towards a chair.

'Your turn to sit down while I make us both a coffee.'

She did as she was told. 'Bryony always used to talk about the mountains,' she said, suddenly eager to change the subject. She didn't want to dwell on David. 'She really missed them when she was in London.'

Oliver nodded. 'Most people who are born here end up coming back. The mountains are in the blood.'

Helen took the coffee he handed her with a smile of thanks. 'I certainly don't feel as though London is in my blood,' she confessed ruefully. 'It's been my home all my life, but I'm not missing it at all.'

But perhaps that was because of everything that had happened.

Oliver sat down opposite her and shot her a curious look. 'Are you not? Well, perhaps we'll convert you to our rural, heathen ways after all. And tomorrow you'll find out what it's like to work in a small GP practice. I hope you like it.'

Helen felt a frisson of anxiety. She was sure she'd like it. But what if she didn't have the necessary skills? Oliver teased her about being a city girl, but what if she just didn't fit into his practice?

She gave herself a sharp talking-to.

He'd been so kind to her and he needed help, she reminded herself firmly. And she'd help him or die in the attempt.

CHAPTER FIVE

THE practice was light and airy, set in a modern building with a huge glass atrium that allowed spectacular views of the mountains.

Helen stared in awe out of the window of the consulting room that she'd been allocated. 'It's so beautiful. How am I ever expected to get any work done?'

'You keep your back to the window,' Oliver advised, flinging open some cupboards to show her where everything was kept. 'We've got everything you're likely to need. If you can't find something, press two on your telephone and that puts you straight through to Pam on Reception. Hit this button on your computer...' he tapped with a long finger '...and you can access your list for the day and the patient records.'

Helen was surprised. 'It's all very high tech.'

'We may be rural but we're not backward.' Oliver's gaze slid down over her figure and a faint frown touched his dark brows. 'That uniform is loose on you,' he said softly, his eyes lifting to hers. 'Ellie is pretty small so I think that means you've lost weight.'

Helen straightened the uniform self-consciously, knowing that he was right. The uniform *was* loose.

'Maybe I could advertise it as a new diet,' she joked feebly. 'The Break-Up Diet. Lose half a stone in two weeks.'

He didn't laugh. 'I'm going to tell Pam to make

sure you eat lunch. I'd force-feed you myself but I have a meeting that I can't get out of. But I'll see you tonight at dinner. And I'm cooking.'

With that he left the room, returning moments later with his two partners who both greeted her warmly and thanked her for helping out.

'Maggie does an asthma clinic on a Monday morning,' Ally Nicholson told her. 'Are you OK with that?'

'Definitely.' Helen nodded immediately. 'Asthma was a real problem in the inner-city practice where I worked. I've done the training course and I'm used to running clinics. If I have any worries, I'll call one of you.'

Obviously satisfied that she was going to be able to cope, the other two GPs hurried off to start their morning surgeries and Oliver gave a satisfied nod.

'You're going to be fine,' he said softly. 'Just don't forget to eat.'

Halfway through her asthma clinic Oliver stuck his head around her door. 'I've got a patient I need some help with. I need a different perspective.'

'Go on.'

Having established that she didn't have anyone with her, he walked into the room and closed the door behind him.

'She's another one of my big worries.'

'Oliver, you worry about all your patients,' Helen pointed out calmly, and he grinned.

'I know. But I really worry about this one. She's seventeen and she has asthma but refuses to acknowledge it. The registrar at the hospital just called me. Apparently she was admitted on Friday after a nasty attack but even that wasn't enough to motivate her to do something about her disease. They sounded pretty infuriated with her.'

'That's not very helpful.' Helen looked at him thoughtfully. 'Teenagers have very special needs. Does she have a management plan?'

'In theory. I suspect in practice her management plan involves ignoring her asthma until it's time to call the ambulance.'

Helen sighed. 'I'll talk to her. Is she outside now?'

Oliver nodded. 'With her mother, who is wringing her hands and clearly hasn't slept for two days.'

'Oh, dear.' Helen looked at the list on her computer. 'Well, my next patient hasn't arrived so I could see her now. But can we leave the mother in the waiting room? If we're having a proper conversation about things that matter to teenagers, I suspect it won't be helpful to have her mother in the room.'

'I'll deal with it. Thanks.'

Oliver vanished and then reappeared moments later. Behind him loitered a slim girl with an extremely sulky expression on her pretty face.

'Anna, this is Helen.' Oliver nudged the girl gently into the consulting room. 'She's from London.'

'London?' The girl looked at Helen with an envious expression on her face. 'You lucky thing. I'd do anything to go and live in London. Actually, I'd do anything to live anywhere but here.'

Oliver looked at Helen helplessly and she smiled. 'I expect you have patients to see, Dr Hunter.'

'I do.' He gave her a grateful smile and left the room.

'That man is seriously cool. He could give me the kiss of life any day.' Anna stared after Oliver with a wistful expression on her face and then turned back to Helen. 'I suppose you're going to lecture me, so you might as well make a start.'

'Is that what you think people do?'

'All the time.' Anna slouched in her chair, her expression defiant. 'It's always, "Anna have you done your peak flow?" or, "Anna have you got your inhaler?" just before I go clubbing. And it's always while my friends are standing there.'

'And how does that make you feel?' Helen asked casually.

'Embarrassed. Different. Like some sort of freak.'

'Why don't you tell me what happened on Friday?'

Anna shrugged and picked some imaginary fluff off her sleeve. 'It was hockey. I'm good at hockey. We were winning and then suddenly I couldn't breathe.' She broke off and her eyes filled with tears. 'And the next thing I knew they'd driven an ambulance onto the school field. It was the most humiliating experience of my life.'

'Do you like hockey?'

'Yes, and now I suppose you're going to tell me I can't do it because of my asthma.'

'Not at all.' Helen opened her door and reached for a pad and pen. 'In fact, you shouldn't have to limit your physical activity at all providing your asthma is controlled—but yours obviously isn't. I like your shoes, by the way.'

Anna glanced down at her feet, obviously taken aback. 'You do?'

'They're great. Everyone is wearing them in London.'

Anna looked at her suspiciously. 'You're different

from the usual nurse. She was at school with my mother. You don't look much older than me.'

'I'm twenty-five,' Helen told her, 'so it isn't that long since I was a teenager.'

Anna stared at her for a long moment. 'It isn't just the exercise that gets me.'

'What else?'

'There's this boy.' She bit her lip, her cheeks suddenly flushed. 'He's asked me out a few times but I keep saying no. He's so cool,' Anna breathed, 'but how can I go out with him? He doesn't know I have asthma. Where do I put an inhaler on a date?'

'Well, it depends on the date,' Helen said practically. 'Let's take it one step at a time. Why don't you want him to know you have asthma?'

'He'll think I'm pathetic.'

'Then he's probably not that cool,' Helen said gently. 'And as for where you put the inhaler on a date, what's wrong with your handbag?'

'I don't want anyone to see.'

'The better controlled your asthma, the less likely you are to have an attack like the one last Friday.'

Anna breathed out heavily. 'All right, then. What does it take?'

'We can look at a few things together. We need to monitor your asthma. Do you think you could keep a diary for a couple of weeks? Monitor your peak flow and your symptoms?'

Helen used the pad and paper to illustrate what she was suggesting and talked to Anna about her peak-flow technique.

'And you reckon if I do all that, I can play hockey without dying on the field.'

Helen smiled. 'I would certainly hope so. Why

don't we give it a go? Come back and see me again next week. In the meantime, make a note of everything that's worrying you and we'll chat about it.'

Anna stood up. 'And you think I should say yes to that date?'

'If he's that cool, definitely,' Helen said firmly, and Anna grinned.

'I'll keep you posted.'

'You do that.'

Helen waited until Anna had left the room and then went to find Oliver.

'She basically doesn't seem to use her inhalers at all,' she told him, 'because she's so busy hiding them.'

'So how do we get around that?'

Helen smiled. 'We show her she's going to have a much better life if she isn't breathless.'

Oliver's eyes narrowed. 'You think that will work?'

'It's worth a try. Oh, and, Dr Hunter—' Helen turned with her hand on his door, her eyes twinkling '—you probably ought to know that Anna thinks you're seriously cool.'

Oliver grinned and folded his arms across his chest. 'I *am* seriously cool, Nurse Forrester. Have you only just discovered that?'

Helen laughed and went back to her own consulting room, suddenly glad that she'd agreed to take the job.

She hadn't had time to think about David all morning.

By the end of the week Helen had decided that it was more a question of finding time to eat than remembering.

She was extremely busy, and with such a range of problems that she was constantly challenged.

But, as good as his word, Oliver had given her the four-wheel drive, together with a quick driving lesson, and in her lunch breaks she explored the local area, by car and on foot.

And by the end of the week she'd found a wonderful block of flats which she thought might appeal to Hilda.

'There's a warden,' she told Oliver that night over dinner, 'but she'd be as independent as she wanted to be. And although the view over the lake is amazing, she's still only two minutes' walk from town.'

'I'm not sure if she'd want to live in a flat,' Oliver mused. 'She lives in a house at the moment.'

'And she's really struggling with the stairs,' Helen told him, recalling the conversation she'd had with Hilda earlier that week when she'd come in to have her peak flow and blood pressure checked. 'The house has been her home all her married life and it would be easy to assume that she doesn't want to leave it, but I think she does want to leave it.'

Oliver put down his fork and looked at her. 'Go on.'

'Well, she misses Barry dreadfully.' Helen shrugged helplessly. 'And everything about that house reminds her of him. Obviously, for some people that's a good thing, but for Hilda I don't think that's the case. She doesn't want the constant reminders. She wants to move on.'

'You sound as though you've had quite a chat with her.'

Helen flushed. 'She came in to have her blood pressure checked earlier in the week. She was the last appointment before lunch so I gave her a lift home instead of calling a taxi. She gave me lunch.'

Oliver smiled. 'I'm glad someone is feeding you.' He stifled a yawn. 'I wanted to feed you myself, but it's been a bit of a hairy week. Michelle has been discharged, by the way, and she's doing fine. I popped in to see her at home today. She said to say thank you and she'd love to see your strappy shoes some-time.'

Helen laughed. 'I'll remember to keep them in my boot so that I can show her the next time I'm passing. And, Oliver…' Her smile faded. 'You don't have to feed me. I'm fine.'

He leaned back in his chair, his blue eyes narrowed as they searched her face. 'You're still looking tired and peaky. What you need is fresh air. This weekend I'm taking you into the mountains.'

Helen looked at him with no small degree of con-sternation. 'Oliver, I'm a town person, remember?'

'But you'll be walking with your own personal guide,' he reminded her, a smug expression on his handsome face. 'I will be responsible for every step you take.'

She bit her lip, wondering if she should admit the truth to him. 'Oliver…'

'What?'

'I'm afraid of heights. I mean, seriously afraid of heights.' She broke off and braced herself for his laughter, but instead he reached across the table and slid his hand over hers. It felt warm, strong and very comforting.

'Will you trust me to take you somewhere you won't feel scared?' His gaze warmed her. 'I promise not to leave you stranded on a ledge or make you walk over anything remotely scary.'

Feeling thoroughly embarrassed by her own inadequacy, Helen looked at him uncertainly. 'I don't know why you would want to take me for a walk. There must be lots of people who would keep you company who aren't afraid of heights.'

'The trouble is,' he said slowly, his expression enigmatic, 'I don't want lots of people. I want you.'

His last sentence was ambiguous and her eyes locked on his. 'Oliver...' Her voice was a croak and he gave a lopsided smile and locked fingers with her.

'Stop worrying, little town mouse. You're going to have a good time.'

And suddenly she found that she wasn't thinking about her fear of heights. She was thinking about spending the weekend with Oliver.

They set out early, but only after Oliver had checked every single item of her clothing.

'If you use a layering system when you dress, it will keep you warmer,' he told her, zipping her into his sister's fleece jacket and then handing her an outer shell. 'This is the waterproof, windproof bit. How are those boots?'

Helen wiggled her toes and stamped on the spot. 'They feel fine.'

'We're lucky that they fit you. If they start to rub let me know but Bryony has them pretty well worn in.'

'I feel like Michelin Man.'

'You look great.' He handed her a hat. 'Put this on.'

She pulled a face. 'I don't look that great in hats.'

'Helen.' His tone was patient. 'You are not going

shopping in the King's Road. You are about to brave the elements. Wear the hat.'

She took it from him with a sigh and pulled it onto her head.

He looked at her, his gaze assessing. 'Actually, I disagree. I think you do look great in hats.' He lowered his head and kissed her gently and then turned and picked up a rucksack that looked ridiculously heavy.

Helen stared after him, frozen into stillness by that kiss.

Her whole body tingled even though the contact had been relatively brief.

What had he meant by it?

Why had he kissed her?

And why did she feel so bitterly disappointed that he'd stopped?

Stunned by the thoughts she was having, Helen shook herself. It was natural that she should enjoy the company of an attractive man when her confidence in herself had been so badly rocked. It didn't mean anything. She would have felt the same about anyone who paid her attention.

Why the hell had he kissed her?

Oliver was suffering from a severe case of frustration.

Maybe if he stripped off and rolled in the snow he might be able to cool his aching body, he mused, trying hard to occupy his mind with something—*anything*—that would distract him from the beautiful woman walking behind him.

He'd positioned her behind him because he knew that if she led the way he'd lose all concentration.

She was so sweet and honest.

And the kiss had been a serious mistake.

An impulse which he was now regretting more than he could possibly have imagined because he'd discovered that one relatively chaste kiss was never going to be enough.

He wanted more.

He wanted everything that this woman had to offer.

Which meant that he was in serious trouble because up until two weeks ago she'd been engaged to another man. Three weeks ago, he corrected himself quickly. A whole week had passed and during that time he'd become more and more convinced that David was totally the wrong guy for her.

Somehow he needed her to see that for herself.

He felt her hand tap him on the back and he stopped, turning immediately. 'Are you all right?'

She was out of breath, her cheeks pink with exertion, and he thought he'd never seen a more gorgeous woman in his life. Her eyes sparkled and her soft lips were parted as she gasped for breath.

'Next time I'm going walking with someone with shorter legs.' She took a deep breath and grinned at him. 'You are very fit.'

Oliver had a sudden urge to power her back against the nearest rock and show her just how fit he was.

Instead, he took a step backwards, just in case the temptation to touch her became too great. 'Sorry. My mind was elsewhere.'

'What were you thinking about?'

He shrugged. 'Stuff…' *Her mostly.* 'I'll slow down.' He waved a hand at the scenery. 'So, what do you think of our playground?'

She exhaled slowly, her eyes drifting over the hard

lines of the mountains. 'It's really beautiful,' she said quietly, and he felt a rush of relief.

He didn't care that she was a townie. He didn't care that she wasn't fit enough to keep up with him.

But if she'd hated his mountains he would have cared.

'So, do you want to play that game I told you about?'

She laughed and stamped her feet to keep warm. 'What? Spot the boulder?'

He nodded and grasped her shoulders, turning her slightly. 'We're going to walk over there.'

'Towards that ravine?' She looked at him doubtfully and he smiled.

'In the Lake District we call it a ghyll and, yes, we're going to walk over there. But we'll turn back before the path climbs upwards.'

'Path?' Helen squinted down at her feet. 'What path?'

'The one that's under your feet. Come on.' He turned and started to trudge up the mountain that was as familiar to him as his own kitchen. 'Tell me what you see on the way. Landmarks.'

'Lots of snow.' She giggled and he turned and grabbed her hand, totally unable to resist at least a small degree of physical contact.

'Noticing lots of snow is not going to help you find your way home if you get lost, city girl.' He waited for her to remove her hand and when she didn't, a warm feeling settled inside him. 'How about this rock?'

She was still laughing. 'OK, I've seen it. Hello, rock.'

Oliver was laughing, too, and his grip on her hand

tightened. 'Something makes me think you're not taking this entirely seriously.'

'I'm not going to get lost,' she said simply. 'I'm with you.'

Oliver caught his breath and wondered why it was that fate had chosen to present him with the right woman at the wrong time.

Not that it was the wrong time for him, of course. He was more than ready to settle down but Helen was so blinded by her recent trauma that there was no way she would be ready to consider a new relationship so soon.

Consoling himself with the thought that time was on his side, he kept hold of her hand and they walked steadily uphill. The more she told him about David, the more obvious it was to him that she hadn't been in love with the guy. She'd drifted into the engagement because that had been what everyone had expected.

Given time and distance from her family, he was sure that she'd eventually come to realise that for herself.

It had finally stopped snowing and the sun was shining, and they didn't pass another person.

He stopped at a rocky outcrop. 'This is far enough and we can sit here without getting wet. Let's have something to eat.' He swung the pack off his back and delved inside. 'Are you hungry?'

She sank down onto the rock and gave him a wry smile. 'Oliver, we both know that you're going to make me eat whether I'm hungry or not, so it doesn't really matter what I say, does it?'

He smiled placidly and pulled out a flask of hot

soup. 'Good point.' He poured the soup into two mugs and handed her one.

She shook her head. 'I'm going to be the size of a block of flats by the time I go back to London.'

The sharp pangs of hunger faded at her words. Suddenly he didn't feel like eating.

Time no longer seemed to be on his side.

'You're going back to London?' He must have looked as horrified as he felt because she gave him a strange look.

'Well, of course I am.' She looked confused. 'Why wouldn't I?'

Because his plan relied on her staying here long enough to realise that she had never been in love with David.

'You've got nothing to go back for.'

She stared across the wild mountain scenery in silence and he saw the pain in her face.

Cursing himself for having been so tactless, he rubbed a hand over the back of his neck. 'I'm sorry,' he groaned, but she shook her head.

'Don't be. It's true.' She took a sip of soup. 'I suppose going back to London isn't something I've even thought about. I gave up my job and the house was David's anyway, so coming up here was an escape.'

'So stay here.'

'I can't hide forever, Oliver, no matter how appealing the thought is.' She gave a sad smile. 'For a start, at some point Bryony is going to want her house back.'

'Not necessarily.' Oliver handed her a sandwich. 'Jack Rothwell owns an enormous pile about three miles from the cottage. I'm sure they'll move in there soon enough. That will leave the cottage empty.'

Helen stared at him and he could tell that the idea hadn't even occurred to her before now.

'Live here…' She stared at the mountains again and let out a long breath. 'That would be like a dream.'

'Then stay.'

'Dreams don't always work in real life,' she said sadly. 'For a start, your practice nurse is only gone for a month,' she reminded him, and he rubbed a hand over his face.

'So we'll find you another job. No problem.'

She smiled. 'Oliver, I don't know anyone here.'

'You know Bryony.' His voice was hoarse. 'And you know me.'

His eyes locked with hers and he could see the question in her eyes.

'Oliver…' Her voice was soft and she looked away, clearly feeling awkward. 'I don't… You can't—'

He sighed. 'Look, I'm going to be honest here so when I've had my say you can black my eye. I like you, Helen. A lot.' Major understatement. 'If you weren't suffering from a very unpleasant break up I would have made a move on you a long time ago.'

Surprise flickered in her blue eyes. 'You've only known me for a week.'

'I've always been decisive. Now it's your turn to be honest. Or are you going to tell me that you haven't felt the chemistry between us?'

She gave a little gasp and the colour seeped into her cheeks. But she didn't deny it. In fact, she didn't speak at all, just turned her head and stared across the valley, leaving him with her profile.

And that didn't tell him anything.

'Helen?' His voice was gentle and he stepped around her so that he could see her face. 'I'm not intending to jump on you, sweetheart. I just wanted to point out that it's there.'

Her eyes locked on his, her expression almost puzzled. 'Two weeks ago I was marrying David.'

'Three weeks,' he corrected her firmly. 'It was three weeks ago, Helen.'

She shook her head and gave a little shrug. 'Three weeks. It still doesn't change the fact that I was marrying another man.'

'But you didn't love him.'

She frowned and shook her head. 'I did. I mean, I do.' She bit her lip, her expression troubled. 'I thought I did—now I don't know any more.'

'All right.' Oliver put both hands on her shoulders and forced her to look at him. 'Let's try something. Tell me what you loved about David.'

'That isn't exactly a fair question.'

'Why not?'

She looked at him helplessly. 'Because right now I'm so angry with him I'm finding it hard to remember.'

Oliver gave a slow smile. 'All right, let's try something different. When did you first realise that you were in love with David?'

'I don't know.' She frowned. 'You make it sound as though it's a light-bulb moment. One minute you're not in love and the next minute you are.'

That's exactly how it had been for him. A light-bulb moment.

The moment he'd seen her in the church he'd known.

Oliver looked at her thoughtfully. 'And it wasn't like that for you?'

'I don't know. I've never really thought about it.' She chewed her lip. 'I started going out with David when I was nineteen—he was my first proper boy-friend, so I suppose I just grew to love him over time.'

Oliver's hands dropped from her shoulders. 'You've been going out with him since you were nineteen?'

She stared at him. 'Why is that so shocking?'

Oliver let out a long breath. 'Because that means you must have been with him for years.'

'Six years.' She nodded. 'What's wrong with that?'

'So when did you decide to marry him?'

'I don't know. It just seemed like the logical next step.'

Oliver looked at her searchingly, wondering if she realised what she was saying.

There didn't seem to have been a single grain of romance in her relationship with David.

'What about you?' She looked at him almost de-fiantly. 'You're not married so you're obviously not exactly dedicated to commitment.'

'It is precisely my dedication to commitment that has stopped me from marrying the wrong person,' Oliver said calmly. 'I've been waiting for Miss Right.'

Helen smiled. 'But you've never found her?'

'I found her a week ago.'

There was a long silence and a mixture of shock and excitement flickered across her blue eyes. 'Oliver, you don't—'

'If you're about to tell me that I've only known you for a week, then I should probably remind you that I'm a very decisive person. Always have been. I know what I want, and once I know what I want I make a point of making sure that I get it.'

She swallowed hard, her eyes fixed on his. 'And what do you want, Oliver?'

'You,' he said softly, lifting a hand and cupping her face as he looked down into her eyes. 'I want you, Helen. And I'm prepared to wait until you realise that you want me, too.'

'Oliver…' She tried to pull away but he slid his other hand around her waist and anchored her against him.

'Let's just try something, shall we?'

Holding her gently but firmly, he brought his mouth down on hers.

Her lips were soft and sweet and Oliver gave a groan, waiting for her to pull away or slap his face, but instead she gave a little sigh and her mouth opened under his. His last coherent thought was that kissing Helen was going straight to the top of his list of favourite pastimes and then he sank under the surface of an excitement so intense that it couldn't be measured.

His previously clear mind was drugged by sensation and he kissed her fiercely, driven by a ravenous hunger deep inside him.

He felt her arms slide around his neck and Oliver dragged her closer, frustrated by the thickness of the clothing that separated them, desperate to rip off her layers so that he could feast on her body.

He felt her quiver against him, felt the intensity of her response as she kissed him back, and knew without doubt that this was the woman he was going to spend the rest of his life with.

But he had the sense to know that he couldn't take her there in one enormous leap, and when she suddenly made a little sound and pushed at his chest, he didn't try and stop her.

To be honest, he was too shocked to stop her.

He'd kissed enough women in his life to think that he'd experienced all the different degrees of sexual excitement, but nothing had come close to the way he'd felt kissing Helen. It was as if all the other kisses had been in black and white and this one had been in colour.

And you didn't have to be a genius to know that it had been the same for her.

Her breath was coming in shallow pants and she dropped her eyes, focusing her attention on the middle of his chest. 'I can't believe I just did that.'

'You didn't,' he said calmly. 'I did. I was the one who kissed you.'

'But I kissed you back.'

She sounded so appalled that he smiled.

'Well, just a bit perhaps.'

'Anyone could have seen us.'

'Those sheep over there definitely saw.'

She didn't smile and he gave a sigh and stroked the back of his hand down her cheek in a gesture that was supposed to comfort. 'Is that why you stopped? Because someone might have seen us?'

'Yes. No.' She was deliciously confused and he felt something shift inside him.

'Helen, stop analysing, sweetheart,' he advised softly. 'We kissed and it was—it was…' *What was it?* How on earth did you describe a kiss like that? Explosive? Frightening? 'It was just a kiss.'

She looked at him. 'Two weeks ago I was marrying David.'

'Three weeks ago.' He gritted his teeth. 'It was three weeks ago.'

She gave a lopsided smile. 'You think one more week makes a difference to the fact that I just got carried away with another man?'

'You weren't carried away, Helen,' he said easily. 'You stopped it. If you'd been carried away we'd both now be naked on that rock at severe risk of suffering frostbite.'

She blushed and looked away. 'I can't believe I let you kiss me. That I kissed you back.' Her expression was troubled. 'I've never— I don't know what I was thinking of. Why did I let you?'

'Because I'm irresistible,' he said helpfully, and then sighed when she didn't laugh.

'Relax, sweetheart. It was only a kiss.'

Only for him it hadn't been just a kiss. It had been an affirmation.

'B-but I'm not like that,' she stammered, pushing a strand of dark hair out of her eyes. 'I don't— I mean I've never…'

'You don't go 'round kissing men you find attractive. Well then perhaps it's time you started,' Oliver said, pulling the edges of her jacket together and zipping it up firmly. 'Come on. Let's go home.'

'I can't have an affair with you, Oliver.'

His hands paused on her jacket. 'Have I asked you to?'

'No. But I'm just making it clear that I can't.'

'Why can't you?'

'For a start, I'm seriously on the rebound.' She gave a wan smile. 'I'm completely confused. To be perfectly honest, I don't know how I feel about David anymore but I do know that I'm not a good bet for any man.'

'Then it's a good job I've always been a risk taker,' Oliver said cheerfully, turning away to stuff the rest of the picnic in the rucksack. 'Don't worry about me.'

'I'll hurt you.'

'In case you haven't noticed, I'm pretty tough.' Oliver heaved the rucksack onto his broad shoulders and paced back to her. 'All right, this is what we're going to do. Call it your rehabilitation programme. You're going to carry on working for me, we're going to carry on living together. You're going to carry on recovering from David and we're going to carry on kissing whenever we feel like it and see where it leads us.'

'It won't lead anywhere. In a few weeks I'll be going back to London.'

'Right.' Oliver gave a bland smile and started down the path, wondering what she'd say if she knew that he had no intention of ever letting her return to London again.

He was going to marry her.

CHAPTER SIX

HELEN'S thoughts were so jumbled up for the rest of the weekend that it was a relief to return to work on Monday.

She'd spent most of Sunday trying to avoid Oliver, which was virtually impossible in a cottage the size of Bryony's when the man in question was the size of Oliver.

Every time she'd turned around he'd seemed to be watching her with that lazy, sexy look that made her insides feel funny.

And she couldn't stop thinking about that kiss.

She tried to think of a time when a kiss from David had left her so churned up, and failed. In fact, she couldn't even remember what it felt like to kiss David. Maybe it was just because she'd been kissing David since she was nineteen.

But had his kisses ever felt as though she was on the verge of something deliciously exciting? Had she ever wanted his kisses to carry on and on and never stop?

Because that's how she'd felt with Oliver.

Seriously disturbed, Helen tried to apply some logic to her tumbled feelings.

She was feeling emotionally bruised and battered and Oliver Hunter had been extraordinarily kind to her. It was only natural that she should feel drawn to him. It was nothing more than that.

But it felt like a lot more.

'Are you all right, Helen?' Pam, the receptionist, wandered into her room clutching some notes. 'You look miles away.'

'Just thinking.' Helen forced a smile. 'I'm fine. Are those notes for me?'

Pam nodded. 'I know you've got a full clinic already, but Howard Marks has asked if you'll see him.' She frowned. 'He saw Dr Hunter last week and after he came out of his appointment he was hovering around Reception for ages as if he was trying to pluck up courage to say something. That's why I thought you might agree to see him. I've just got a feeling…'

'Of course I'll see him,' Helen said immediately, taking the set of notes from Pam. 'Perhaps I'll just have a quick word with Dr Hunter first before I call him in. Just so that I have some background.'

'Good idea. He's in between patients at the moment and your next one hasn't turned up so you've been blessed with time to breathe.'

'Thanks, Pam.'

Wondering how it was that she could feel so at home in a practice after only a week, Helen walked across the corridor to Oliver's consulting room and tapped on the door.

She heard his deep voice tell her to enter but her hand paused on the door handle as she braced herself to face him. For the whole weekend all she'd been able to think about had been that kiss.

What if she'd lost the ability to work with him professionally?

Just as she was plucking up the courage to open the door, it was tugged open from the inside and Oliver stood there, his blue eyes questioning as they rested on her face.

'Is something wrong?'

Her eyes dropped to his firm mouth and she forced herself to lift her gaze and look him in the eyes. Something flickered deep in his eyes and then he stood to one side to let her in.

'I wanted to talk about a patient,' she said quickly, just in case he thought she'd knocked on his door with something more personal in mind. 'Someone called Howard Marks has asked to see me. Apparently he saw you last week. I just wondered if you could give me a bit of background.'

Oliver frowned and folded his arms across his chest. 'Howard has asked to see you? I can't imagine what for...' He was silent for a moment and then shook his head. 'No idea. He's a very heavy smoker and he suffers from emphysema. He developed a chest infection over Christmas so I gave him antibiotics. I checked his chest last week and it was free of infection. End of story.'

'That's fine. I just wanted to check that there wasn't anything I should know before I saw him.'

Oliver shook his head. 'Howard is a great guy. He was a friend of my father's—I've known him since I was tiny.'

'Have you?' Helen tilted her head to one side and looked at him thoughtfully. 'I wonder whether that's why he wants to see me.'

'What do you mean?'

'Nothing.' She smiled and walked towards the door. 'Just a thought, and I'm probably wrong anyway so it's stupid to voice it. I'll catch you later, Oliver.'

Suddenly she was breathlessly aware of his broad shoulders and the hard muscle of his thighs outlined by the soft fabric of his trousers. He had a powerful, very masculine physique and without too much effort on her part she could remember just how it had felt to be pressed close to his body.

And she needed to get herself away from his body as fast as possible so that she could somehow regain control of her mind.

Not daring to analyse what was happening to her, she hurried back to the sanctuary of her room and closed the door firmly behind her.

To begin with work had provided a distraction from David. Now it seemed to be providing a distraction from Oliver as well.

She pressed the buzzer to call her next patient and then smiled as a tall, pale-looking man walked into her room.

'Mr Marks? I'm Helen Forrester. Please, have a seat.'

He closed the door carefully and sat down opposite her, his fingers playing nervously in his lap.

'What can I do for you, Mr Marks?'

He shifted awkwardly in his chair and then ran a hand over the back of his neck. 'I have this thing called emphysema…'

Helen nodded. 'Yes. I read your notes. How are you getting on?'

'Well, not great, to be honest.' He pulled a face. 'I have to breathe in that blessed oxygen sixteen hours a day and then at Christmas I managed to catch something horrible and I was back in bed, coughing my guts up.'

'But the antibiotics that Dr Hunter gave you cleared that up?'

'Oh, ay.' He nodded and glanced at her briefly before looking away again. 'He's a good doctor is young Oliver.'

Helen looked at him thoughtfully. 'And you've known him all your life.'

'Knew his father and mother before they were married.' Howard Marks gave a short laugh. 'Can't believe Oliver is grown up, to be honest.'

'It must be a bit difficult, talking to him about some things,' Helen volunteered, keeping her voice casual, and when he met her eyes she knew that she was right.

'He's a brilliant doctor,' the man said quickly, 'but I remember him as a kid. How can I talk to him about—about—' He broke off and Helen gave a nod.

'About something really personal,' she finished gently, and Howard sighed.

'Stupid, isn't it, really? An old fool like me.'

'If something is worrying you, you should talk about it. Is that why you asked to see me, Mr Marks? Because I'm a stranger?'

He gave her a keen look. 'You're not stupid, are you?'

'I hope not.' Helen smiled. 'And I do understand that it's easier to talk to a stranger about some things.'

'I thought that. That's why I asked to see you.' He broke off and gave a long sigh. 'And now I'm here I don't know how to say it. You'll think I'm completely ridiculous.'

Helen shook her head. 'I won't think that. If the problem is serious enough to bring you here then it's serious enough for me to take it seriously.'

He glanced towards the door as if he was contemplating running through it. 'Your next patient is probably waiting.'

'Then they can wait a bit longer,' Helen said calmly. 'Please, trust me, Mr Marks. Tell me what's worrying you and we'll try and find a solution together.'

'I'm sixty-six,' he wheezed. 'Been married for forty-two years and we've always had a good—well, we've always enjoyed—'

'Sex?' Helen's voice was calm. 'Has it become a problem, Mr Marks?'

He slumped in his chair and ran a hand over his face. 'I can't believe I'm discussing it with you. You're younger than my daughter.'

'But I'm also a professional who cares about your health,' Helen reminded him, 'and sexuality is part of health. If it's any consolation, plenty of patients have discussed exactly the same issue with me. It's very common, particularly in patients who are suffering from respiratory conditions like you.'

He looked at her. 'You've talked to other patients about this?'

'Absolutely. In London there are specialist nurses who deal with this area.'

He gave an embarrassed smile. 'When you get to my age you assume that people think you don't have sex any more.'

'Sex is an important part of a relationship,' Helen said quietly. 'Do you want to tell me exactly what the problem is?'

He rubbed a hand over his face. 'Well, I just run out of energy. And I suppose I'm frightened because I get breathless.'

'Do you leave your oxygen on when you make love?'

He frowned and shook his head. 'No, of course not.'

'It would probably help if you did. Do you ever go for walks?'

'Sometimes, but I always use my puffer before exercise and that seems to do the trick.'

Helen nodded. 'Treat making love as you would any other exercise,' she advised. 'Have a puff of your bronchodilator before and keep the oxygen on. Have a rest before you make love and it might be wise to avoid alcohol because that can actually inhibit sexual arousal.'

'What about the fact that I get breathless? It scares the wife.'

'Shortness of breath while you're making love is entirely normal,' Helen said simply. 'As long as you are feeling OK you shouldn't worry about it.'

'The wife thinks I'm going to drop dead.'

'Then you can assure her that sudden death during intercourse is extremely uncommon.' Helen reached for her diary and a piece of paper. 'There's a really good leaflet that outlines some sexual positions which help you conserve energy. I used to have a few in the place where I worked last but if you call this number they can send you a copy. In the meantime, this is what I suggest.'

She talked frankly for a few minutes more and then Howard rose to his feet and gave her a grateful smile.

'I can't thank you enough. I feel a lot better.'

'Good.' Helen stood up and walked him to the door. 'Anytime you have any worries just pop back and see me.'

And then she remembered that the chances were she wouldn't be here.

Her life was in London.

She buzzed for her next patient, a frown on her face.

If she was honest with herself she was enjoying this small community where everyone knew about everyone else.

And she was enjoying working with Oliver.

She sucked in a breath and stared out of the window, her eyes on the snow-covered fells that he loved so much.

It was still troubling her that she was becoming so obsessed with Oliver when only a few weeks before she'd been making preparations to spend the rest of her life with David.

It was just self-preservation, she assured herself, pulling herself together as her next patient tapped on her door. David had rejected her so brutally that it was perfectly natural for her to respond when an attractive man flirted with her.

And Oliver wasn't serious. She knew he couldn't be serious.

He'd only known her for just over a week.

That afternoon she finished work on time and went and collected Hilda from her cottage.

'I just want to show you something,' she said, waiting while Hilda picked up her coat and bag. 'And, anyway, it'll be fun to get out and have some fresh air. I've been stuck in a surgery surrounded by germs all morning.'

Hilda smiled. 'I see Dr Hunter has leant you his four-by-four.'

'That's right.' Helen grinned and opened the passenger door for her. 'Although why he trusts us girls with it, I have no idea.'

Hilda laughed and climbed into the vehicle with some discreet help from Helen. 'I suppose this is the point where you tell me you used to be a racing driver.'

'Would you mind if I was?'

'Not at all.' Hilda fastened her seat-belt. 'To be honest, I'm in the market for some excitement.'

'Well, you can relax. I'm not that confident with his car yet,' Helen confessed ruefully, pulling out and setting off towards the town. 'So we'll have to seek our excitement in other directions.'

'So how are you settling down, dear?'

'Very well. Everyone is very kind.'

Hilda glanced across at her. 'And you're living with Dr Hunter…'

Helen blushed. 'We're both staying in his sister's house. I wouldn't exactly say I'm living with him.'

'Sounds as though you're living with him to me,' Hilda said placidly, reaching down and picking up her bag. 'And a good thing, too. We've all waited a long time to see Oliver find the right woman.'

Helen gave a soft gasp. 'Hilda, I'm not the right woman.'

'Judging from the way he was looking at you when he brought you to my house that first weekend, I think he might have a different opinion on that subject.'

Helen shook her head. 'I've known him for less than two weeks.'

'I fell in love with my husband in two minutes,' Hilda said wistfully, pulling a tissue out of her bag and blowing her nose. 'And he was the same. When you know, you know.'

'I probably ought to tell you that until very recently I was engaged to another man.' Helen tightened her fingers on the steering-wheel, wondering why she was disclosing intimate details of her private life to a patient. 'I shouldn't be telling you this…'

'Why not? It does me good to hear about other peoples' lives,' Hilda said calmly. 'Stops me brooding on my own problems. So what happened?'

'He ended it the day before the wedding. He phoned from the airport as he was about to board a plane.' For the first time since it had happened, Helen was able to assess David's behaviour objectively. 'What a rat.'

'A coward of the worse kind,' Hilda agreed fervently, 'but he did you a favour, dear. Whatever pain you might be feeling now, it's nothing compared to waking up every day next to a man you don't love. And there's no way a sweet girl like you could have been in love with a man who could behave like that.'

'I thought I was.'

'Everyone can make a mistake.' Hilda peered curiously out of the window. 'I've never been down this road before. Where are we?'

'If you turn right at the end of the road you end up at the edge of the lake. It's very pretty. And the flat has lovely views of the lake from the sitting room and the main bedroom.'

Hilda looked at her. 'What flat?'

'The flat I'm taking you to see.' Helen bit her lip nervously. 'Please, don't make a judgement until you've seen it. Oliver thinks you won't want to leave the home you lived in with Barry all your life, but I think that home is full of memories for you. Some good, some too painful to live with on a daily basis. I wondered whether you might want to think about a fresh start. Make some new memories somewhere else. And this is a pretty good place to do it. Will you at least look at it?'

There was a long silence while Hilda stared out of the window and then she stirred herself. 'Of course I'll look at it.'

Breathing a huge sigh of relief, Helen switched off the engine.

The warden was waiting for them and Hilda gave a huge smile. 'Well, it's Cathy Janson. How are you, my dear?'

'Brilliant.' Cathy gave the older woman a hug and jangled some keys. 'I didn't realise that it was you who was interested in the flat. It would be fantastic having you living here.'

Helen glanced from one to the other. 'Obviously you know each other.'

'I was the headmistress of the local primary school,' Hilda told her with a wistful smile. 'I taught Cathy. It was a long time ago. She always wore her hair in pigtails then.'

Cathy smiled. 'Come and see the flat.'

She unlocked the door for them and Hilda went first, walking straight to the huge picture window that overlooked the lake. Several boats were moored at a tiny jetty and even though it was bitterly cold, people were strolling along the path that weaved its way along the side of the lake. Behind the lake the mountains rose, filling the background.

'What an amazing view.' Finally Hilda moved, glancing around her with obvious approval. 'And what a lovely warm room. There are times when I think I'm going to freeze to death in my cottage at the moment. The wind seems to howl through every crack. Show me the rest.'

By the time they'd looked around and sat in the living room while Hilda stared at the view, an hour had passed.

Cathy stood up. 'I'm going to have to leave you because I'm picking my Nicky up from school. Just post the keys back through my letter-box when you've finished.' She put a hand on Hilda's shoulder. 'I was so sorry to hear about Barry.'

Hilda let out a breath. 'Life sends us trials and we have to face them. For a while I didn't think I could. But now I think this might be the answer. Change. Something new.'

Cathy and Helen exchanged looks and Cathy made for the door. 'I'll be hearing from you, then.'

The door closed behind her and Hilda stirred. 'Thank you.'

'For what?'

'For daring to suggest what no one else would. The home that I've lived in all my life just doesn't feel like home now that Barry isn't in it with me. If I move here, I can walk the short distance to town, I can chat to Cathy and help pick her daughter up from school. And when it's too cold to go out I can still watch life from this amazing window.'

Helen smiled, a huge feeling of relief washing over her. 'So you want it?'

'Definitely. How hard will it be to arrange everything?'

'Well, you'll need to sell your house.'

'That will be easy enough. The couple next door

have been dying to buy it for years. They want to knock the two cottages into one big house. I'll talk to them when I get home. And I'll call Cathy. My son can help me with the details.'

A week later, Hilda had made an offer on the flat and instructed her solicitor to sell her cottage to the couple next door.

On Friday evening Oliver cooked Helen dinner and they cracked open a bottle of wine.

'In three weeks you seem to have sorted out the whole community.' Oliver raised his glass, an odd smile playing around his firm mouth. 'I couldn't believe that Anna actually came back to see you.'

'Twice, actually. In each case complete with diary and peak-flow readings,' Helen said happily, recalling her discussion with the teenager. 'And, more importantly, she's got a date tomorrow.'

'A date?' Oliver blinked. 'How do you know about her love life?'

'Because her love life is actually an important key to her asthma management,' Helen said simply. 'She didn't want the boy to know she was asthmatic. Anyway, she told him yesterday and it turns out that his sister is asthmatic so suddenly everything is rosy. She's going clubbing with him and she even brought her outfit to show me and we found a great place to tuck her inhaler.'

Oliver shook his head. 'You amaze me.' His eyes gleamed wickedly. 'Although I have to confess that someone did warn me that you are the local expert on sexual positions.'

Helen blushed but she held his gaze. 'My conversations with my patients are confidential.'

'They should be,' Oliver agreed dryly, topping up her wine, 'but I have to warn you that it often doesn't stay that way in a small community. According to Howard Marks, you're a cross between Florence Nightingale and—'

'I don't think I want to hear the rest,' Helen interrupted him hastily, her cheeks still pink. 'I just gave him some advice. He didn't want to talk to you because he's known you since you were in nappies. But clearly he didn't mind talking about it afterwards.'

Oliver grinned. 'Man talk. You know how it is.'

Helen rolled her eyes. 'Spare me.'

Oliver's smile faded. 'And thank you for what you've done for Hilda. You wouldn't believe how many sleepless nights I've had over her. I've known her all my life and it just didn't occur to me that she'd want to move. What made you think of it?'

Helen pushed a piece of salmon around her plate. 'The way I feel about moving here, I suppose. When a place is full of memories, it's good to leave it.'

Oliver's blue eyes searched hers. 'So does that mean that you're throwing away your stilettos and staying here?'

In another week Bryony would be back from her honeymoon and Oliver's practice nurse would be back from Australia.

'I don't know.' Helen pulled a face. 'I don't even want to think about it, to be honest. I love it here so much.' She poked her salmon with her fork. 'This is starting to feel like home. I like the people. I like the way their priorities are different.'

'So stay.'

She sighed. 'It isn't that simple, is it?'

'Why not?'

She poked her salmon again. 'Because it feels like running away.' She pulled a face. 'I mean, I know that's exactly what I've done, but sooner or later I have to go home and face the music.'

'Why? Life can be enough of an endurance test without making it worse.' Oliver frowned. 'And what has that salmon ever done to you? You've chopped it into pieces.'

Helen put down her fork and stared at the food on her plate. 'I'm not that hungry.' She looked at him. 'It's funny really. I always had a very clear vision of the way my life would be…'

'And how was that?' Oliver lounged back in his chair and she gave a slight shrug.

'Big house, lots of entertaining, children…'

Oliver gave a twisted smile. 'The corporate wife.'

'I suppose so.'

'And was that your vision or your parents'?'

Helen looked at him, startled. It was a question she'd never asked herself before. 'I suppose I was brought up to think that my life would be like my mother's.'

'So who made the decision to marry David?' Oliver asked evenly. 'You or your parents?'

Helen frowned. 'Me, of course.'

Oliver's expression didn't flicker. 'How did you meet him?'

'He worked for my dad.'

Oliver gave a wry smile. 'And he was deemed a suitable partner for the boss's daughter?'

Helen flushed. 'Something like that. But I liked David.'

'But you don't marry someone because you like them,' Oliver said softly, leaning forward and trapping her eyes with his. 'You marry them because you love them. Did you love him, Helen?'

There was a long silence and she was suddenly aware of the steady beat of her heart and the heat in his eyes.

'I don't know.' She swallowed hard. 'A week ago I would have answered definitely yes, of course I would. If I hadn't loved him, I wouldn't have agreed to marry him.'

'Wouldn't you?' Oliver's gaze was steady on hers. 'You're a sweet girl, Helen. It strikes me that you spend a lot of time doing things for other people. Who were you marrying David for? You or your parents?'

She shook her head. Suddenly the only things she could think about were his unbelievably thick, dark lashes and the lazy, sexy look in his eyes.

'I don't know.' Her voice was barely a whisper and he gave a soft curse and pushed his chair away from the table.

'Oliver?'

He strode around to her side and dragged her to her feet, his mouth descending on hers with a fierce passion that took her by surprise.

She melted instantly, loving the feel of his hard body against hers, this time without the frustrating barrier of outdoor clothing.

As kisses went, this one was crazy, a desperate, driven explosion of sexual chemistry that was stronger than both of them.

'You're driving me nuts,' Oliver groaned against her mouth, one strong hand sliding into the softness of her hair, anchoring her head for his kiss. The other arm dragged her closer still, trapping her against the hardness of his arousal. 'Living and working with you is driving me nuts.'

She gasped and pressed closer still and he slid her uniform up her thighs and lifted her in an easy movement, his mouth still on hers as he sat her on the table. Then he slid both hands over her bottom and tugged her close so that her legs were wrapped around him.

He gave a moan of pure masculine appreciation and reluctantly dragged his mouth away from hers, but only so that he could kiss his way down her neck.

'Have I ever told you that you have fabulous legs?' His voice was husky with passion and his strong hands slid purposefully up her thighs, caressing the smooth skin with deliberate strokes, 'because you have totally, amazing legs—I love your legs.'

'*Oliver…*'

His mouth smothered her broken plea for satisfaction and she felt the burning heat of his body against hers, felt the warm seduction of his lips and tongue, the skilled touch of his hands. With a moan of frustration she tugged his shirt out of his trousers and her hands slid underneath, exploring warm, male flesh and hard muscle. He had an incredible physique. Suddenly she wanted to feel all of him and she didn't resist when she felt his fingers impatiently freeing the buttons on her dress.

When his fingers slid beneath her flimsy bra and claimed a nipple she gave a tortured gasp and arched against him, feeling the insistent throb of his arousal pressed hard against her, and when he bent his head and replaced his fingers with his mouth she sobbed with a mixture of pleasure and arousal.

Bells rang in her head, loud and insistent, and it

was only when Oliver lifted his head with a reluctant groan that she realised that it was the phone.

His breath fractured and his eyes slightly dazed, Oliver slowly released her. 'I've got to answer that,' he said hoarsely, pulling the edges of her dress together with visible reluctance. 'I'm on call.'

Unable to move or think clearly, Helen waited until he'd eased away from her and then tugged her uniform down her thighs, her face scarlet as she reviewed her own behaviour.

What had she been thinking of?

She'd been all set to marry David and yet here she was, only a month later, virtually making love with a man on his kitchen table. And the power of her own response to Oliver shocked her. Never before had she experienced one tenth of the urgency, the need, the *desperation* that she'd experienced with Oliver.

If the phone hadn't rung…

Utterly shocked and confused, Helen fastened her buttons quickly, wondering what had happened to her.

Until tonight she'd never thought of herself as a particularly sexual person. In all her years with David, she'd never felt an overwhelming need for sex. They'd kissed, of course, and made love, but it had always been a very dignified experience, whereas she and Oliver…

They'd virtually ripped each other's clothes off.

Oliver was talking on the phone, asking pointed questions and scribbling a few notes on a pad. When he finally replaced the phone he seemed to have recovered some of his composure. But he kept his eyes on the notepad.

'That was one of my pregnant mums. Lily Henderson.' His voice still sounded gruff and he cleared his throat and ran a hand over the back of his neck as he studied his notes.

Perhaps he wasn't so composed after all.

'She's having severe pains but she doesn't think she's in labour.'

Helen made a valiant attempt at normal conversation. 'Shouldn't she go straight to hospital?'

'Yes, but she had a hideous time with her first one—born down south somewhere—and she's determined to have this one at home.'

'Oh, dear.'

'She only moved to the area a month ago and I haven't managed to persuade her to meet Tom, which was what I had in mind.' Oliver drew in a breath, cursed softly and finally looked at her, his gaze acknowledging what had happened between them. 'I've never had trouble concentrating on my job before.'

Her own breathing was suddenly shallow as she connected with those intense blue eyes. 'So are you going to do a visit?'

Her voice sounded disconnected from the rest of her body. As if somehow it were trying to distance itself from the confusing spiral of emotions that were inside her.

'Yes. I'll take a look at her and try and persuade her to go in. But I was talking about us.' His eyes held hers. 'Or are you going to pretend that that kiss didn't happen?'

She swallowed hard. If only it were that easy.

'Oliver—'

'Because it's probably only fair to warn you that I'm not going to let you.' His voice was soft but grimly determined. He ripped the piece of paper from the pad and tucked it into his pocket. 'I know you think that you're on the rebound but I'm not going to let you dismiss this thing between us just because we've only known each other for two weeks. What we have is too special. When we get back from seeing Lily, we're going to talk about this.'

Her stomach lurched and she looked at him helplessly. 'There's no point. I wouldn't know what to say. All I know is that I've never behaved like that with anyone before. You must think I'm...' She covered her face with her hands, just mortified, and felt him gently tug her hands away.

'You really want to know what I think of you?' His eyes darkened and his gaze dropped to her mouth for a lingering moment. 'On second thoughts, this is not the time to have that conversation. Pretty soon I'm going to tell you what I think of you, Helen,' he promised hoarsely, 'but not two minutes before we go to see a patient.'

He was standing so close to her that she could feel the warmth and strength of his body, see the rough stubble on his hard jaw.

'You want me to come with you?'

He gave her that boyish smile that never failed to charm her. 'I could do with some moral support.'

It was late, she was tired but suddenly all she wanted was to be with Oliver. 'All right.'

Some of the tension seemed to leave him. 'Good. Let's go. She lives in a village on the other side of town.' He grabbed his coat and bag and then turned to look at her, a strange gleam in his blue eyes. 'And, Helen—' his voice was soft '—when we come back, we're having that conversation.'

She stared at him, too confused by her own response to answer him.

She'd thought that the only man in the world for her was David, but suddenly the only man on her mind was Oliver.

CHAPTER SEVEN

LILY HENDERSON opened the door to them but it was obvious that she was in severe pain.

'You should be lying down,' Oliver scolded, and she gave him a weary smile.

'How? I've just put the other one to bed and Nick isn't home yet. I've rung him. He's on his way. Come into the sitting room.'

She flopped down on the sofa and took a deep breath. 'Something's not right, Dr Hunter I can feel it. This pain isn't right.'

'You've been in labour before, Lily,' Oliver said calmly. 'Does the pain feel like labour pain?'

She shook her head and pulled a face, rubbing a hand over her swollen abdomen to ease the discomfort. 'No. It doesn't feel like labour pain. It feels like something else. But it isn't good. I'm not going into hospital, Dr Hunter. *I'm not going.*'

'Let's not worry about that at the moment.' Oliver grabbed the sonicaid. 'I just want to listen to the baby's heart, and then we'll talk about our options.'

Seconds later the steady, rhythmic pounding of the baby's heart echoed through the room and Lily gave a soft sigh.

'Oh, I'm so glad to hear that.'

Oliver nodded and switched off the machine. 'Your baby's fine at the moment, Lily, but any pain that bothers you that much should be investigated and I can't do that properly at home. You should be scanned and examined.'

Lily shook her head. 'No.'

'We have a brilliant maternity unit here,' Oliver said softly, 'and it has one of the lowest rates of intervention in the country.'

Lily looked at him, her eyes suddenly frightened. 'You know I don't want to go in. I want to have this baby at home.'

Oliver sighed and ran long fingers through his hair. 'I know you had a bad experience with your last delivery, Lily, but you were just unlucky. You never were anybody's idea of a good candidate for home birth, you know that. And you're even less so now.'

Lily's mouth tightened and Helen saw the sparkle of tears in her eyes. 'The doctors didn't know what they were doing,' she muttered. 'You said you'd deliver me at home if you had to. You and the midwife.'

'And if I have to, I will, but how much of a risk are you willing to take with this baby, Lily?' Oliver's voice was soft. 'I can promise that whatever happened to you last time won't happen this time. I'm going to call my brother. He's the consultant there—remember, I've told you about him? I've told him about you, too.'

'But I don't know him.'

'Fortunately, I've known him for thirty-four years,' Oliver said easily, rising to his feet in a fluid movement and reaching for his phone. 'And he is going to take the very best care of you and this baby.'

Lily started to cry and Oliver gave a soft curse.

'Make your phone call,' Helen said quickly, sliding her arms around Lily and giving her a hug. 'Lily, why don't you tell me what happened last time?'

'He didn't even talk to me,' Lily sobbed, her hand covering her mouth. 'That doctor just strode into the room, yanked the baby out with forceps and left again without saying a single word. He was horrible! And I was in agony for months and months. I couldn't sit for six weeks I was so bruised, and I had to have ultrasound and everything—I just couldn't enjoy the baby.'

Helen winced and hugged her tighter. 'You poor, poor thing,' she said gently. 'But you were just really unlucky, Lily. There is no way Tom Hunter would let that happen.' She didn't even know Tom, but if he was even half as good a doctor as his brother he would be a brilliant obstetrician. 'Trust Dr Hunter, Lily. And think of the baby.'

At that moment the front door flew open and Lily's husband flew in, breathless and visibly stressed.

'Are you all right, pet?' He scooted across the room to his wife and looked at Helen with anxious eyes. 'What's happening?'

'I'm trying to persuade her to go to hospital,' Oliver said, flipping his phone shut and walking over to them. 'I've talked to Tom and he's going to meet us at the hospital. We're going there now.'

'I can't leave Bruce.'

'I've called your mum,' Nick said quickly. 'She's on her way over.'

Lily bit her lip and looked at Oliver. 'Do you promise it won't go wrong?'

Oliver sighed and dropped to his haunches beside her, his handsome face serious. 'What I can promise is that there is no better person than Tom to deliver a baby.'

'But if you were married, would you let him deliver your wife's baby?'

Oliver smiled. 'Oh, yes.'

Helen had a sudden painful vision of Oliver with a pregnant wife and felt a sudden stab of pain in her chest.

He would make a wonderful husband and an even more wonderful father.

Thoroughly unsettled by her own thoughts, Helen forced herself to concentrate on the situation.

Lily looked at him for a long moment and then gave a sniff. 'All right…'

'Good girl.' Oliver straightened in a smooth movement and looked at her husband. 'Has she got a bag packed?'

Lily shook her head. 'No. I didn't bother because I was so determined not to go in.'

Nick slid an arm around her shoulders. 'It'll be all right, babe,' he said firmly, giving Oliver a nod. 'If Dr Hunter trusts his brother, so should we. I'll pack you a bag and I'll follow you to the hospital as soon as your mother arrives.'

Tom Hunter met them in the labour ward. Dressed in green theatre scrubs, he looked broad-shouldered and handsome, a more serious version of his brother.

'Hello, Lily.' He smiled at his patient, his voice surprisingly gentle. 'I gather you had a rotten time of it when you had your last child. Let's try and do better, shall we?' He lifted his eyebrow towards his brother. 'Need my help, do you Oliver?'

'Someone's got to keep your ego intact,' Oliver replied smoothly, winking at Lily. 'You'd better look after my patient or you'll have me to deal with.'

'Very professional, I'm sure.' Tom jerked his head

towards a midwife who was hovering. 'Emma, can you settle Lily in, please? I'll be there in five minutes.'

Oliver turned to Lily and gave her a smile. 'You're going to be fine,' he said firmly. 'I'll see you soon.'

Emma took them down the corridor and Tom looked at Oliver. 'That woman should never have been promised a home delivery.'

Oliver met his gaze full on. 'She's seriously terrified, Tom. It was the only reason I was given access to her house. She's only been in the area for a month. I've promised her that you're the best and nothing will go wrong.'

'No pressure, then,' Tom drawled, taking a chart from a hovering midwife. 'Obstetrics is nothing if not unpredictable, as you well know. Promising a fairy-tale birth might not have been the best approach.'

'You would have rather she bolted the door from the inside and did it by herself?' Oliver's tone was hard. 'Because that's what she would have done, Tom. And she doesn't need a fairy-tale. She just needs to feel that there's someone she can trust. The last guy didn't even speak to her.'

Tom winced. 'Weird, these southerners.' He checked the chart and handed it back to the midwife with a nod. 'That's fine. Call Rob and ask him to come up here, will you? I'm going to be tied up with Lily.'

Oliver let out a sigh of relief. 'You're going to deliver her yourself? Do you promise?'

'I'm not a midwife,' Tom said mildly. 'I'm the guy who steps in when things go wrong. You'd be better with a midwife.'

Oliver shook his head. 'You've got the best instincts of any doctor I've met. If you keep an eye on her all the way through, nothing is going to go wrong.'

Something flickered in Tom's eyes as he looked at his brother. 'Your faith in me is touching.'

'You're the best.' Oliver gave a lopsided smile. 'Arrogant, smug, stubborn and totally self-absorbed, but still the best when it comes to delivering babies.'

Tom laughed. 'I can live with that.' His gaze flickered to Helen and his eyes gleamed wickedly. 'How's your roof coming along, Oliver?'

'Slowly.'

'Of course it is.' For some reason that Helen couldn't fathom, Tom's smile widened and he clapped his brother on the shoulder again. 'All right, I'm off to give your Lily the dream delivery. You owe me a pint. I'll meet you in the pub tomorrow night.'

'Done.'

They left the hospital and drove back to the cottage. Oliver was strangely silent and Helen wondered if he was worrying about Lily.

Or was he thinking about that kiss?

Remembering his promise that they were going to talk about it, Helen was suddenly anxious to delay their arrival home.

She didn't want to have the conversation. She didn't know what she was going to say.

'So your brother doesn't approve of home deliveries?' Perhaps if she kept to work, they could both forget about that kiss.

'Of course not.' Oliver's smile was wry. 'He's an obstetrician. He thinks every birth should take place in a hospital no matter what.'

'And you don't agree?'

He gave a shrug. 'I think a proportion of women are perfectly safe delivering at home providing they understand that in certain circumstances they might need a rapid transfer to hospital. In fact, for some women I think it is definitely the preferred option.'

'Like Lily.'

He pulled a face, his expression troubled. 'Not like Lily, actually. Tom's right. She was always a terrible candidate for home birth, but hers is a classic example of the theory not working in practice. On paper she should definitely have been booked for a hospital delivery, but nowhere on paper does it say how severely traumatised the girl was by her first delivery.'

'Why did she have such a bad experience? Were they negligent?'

'Evidently she had a locum doctor who couldn't be bothered or else wasn't sufficiently experienced. Either way he was very heavy-handed with the forceps and made a terrible mess of her insides. When they first moved here they were refusing any medical help at all.'

'Do you think she'll be OK?'

'Providing Tom doesn't get called away to deal with anything urgent, yes.' Oliver smiled. 'My brother is an amazing obstetrician. He's Mr Super-Cool. You should see him in a crisis. He delivered Ellie, the staff nurse who leant you the uniform— Ben's wife. She had a car accident just before Christmas when she was eight months pregnant. Jack and Tom were both amazing. And Tom's always the same. I think he thrives on crisis. While everyone around him is panicking he barely flickers an eyelid.

I'll give him a call later and see how Lily is getting on.'

He pulled up outside the cottage and switched off the engine. For a moment he sat still, staring into the darkness, and then he turned to look at her and tension throbbed between them.

'Helen, we need to talk about what's happening between us.'

Her heart stumbled in her chest. 'Nothing's happening, Oliver. It can't be.'

'Why not?'

'Because five weeks ago I was marrying another man.' But she had to admit that she was thinking less and less of David. Everything had started to blur in her mind. 'It's too soon—we don't even know each other.'

'Yes, we do,' he said softly, sliding a hand behind her head and gently turning her face to his. 'We do know each other, Helen.'

She closed her eyes briefly and shook her head. 'You've been so kind to me. Without you I would have fallen apart.'

Oliver lifted an eyebrow. 'You're suggesting that that episode on the kitchen table was gratitude?'

His voice was husky and masculine and she felt a shiver of excitement pass through her body.

What did this man do to her?

She flushed. 'I can't believe I behaved like that.'

'Well, you did,' Oliver said softly, 'and since it's obvious that you're not in the habit of indulging in rampant sex on the kitchen table I think that should tell you something about the strength of the attraction between us, don't you?'

She stared at him helplessly. 'I don't know what

I'm feeling.' She bit her lip. It would have been so tempting to just fall into his arms and take their relationship to its natural conclusion. But she couldn't do that. Not when everything seemed so muddled. 'I can't promise you anything, Oliver. I'm afraid I'll hurt you.'

'That's my problem.'

'No, it isn't. I would never want to hurt you.' She flushed. 'This just isn't the way things happen. I can't be about to marry one man and then—'

'And then fall for another?' Oliver's voice was soft as he finished her sentence. 'Why not?'

'Well, for a start because we haven't met during normal circumstances. We haven't had a normal relationship.'

There was a hint of amusement in his eyes. 'What's a normal relationship?'

She shrugged helplessly. 'Well, dating, I suppose. Getting to know each other. I went out with David for six years.'

The amusement faded. 'I don't need six years to know that you're the woman for me, Helen. I knew within six seconds.'

His words made her gasp and her heart almost stopped beating. 'Oliver…'

He couldn't possibly mean that.

'Look…' He gave a sigh and slid his fingers through her hair. 'I know that you still haven't sorted out how you feel about David. But sooner or later you're going to realise that he did you a favour. Not the way he did it—that was cruel and cowardly—but what he did. And I happen to think that what you feel for me is real. But I'll hang around while you find that out for yourself and if dating is important to you, then we'll date.'

She was breathlessly aware of every powerful inch of him. 'You said that living and working with me was driving you nuts.'

'And I can think of a very good way of relieving that frustration.' He flashed her a wicked smile. 'But I'm just a simple mountain man. If dating is what it takes then dating is what we'll do. Tomorrow night is quiz night at the Drunken Fox. The pinnacle of our monthly social calendar up here in the wilds. Most of the mountain rescue team should be there. It will rival anything you have in London, city girl.'

At the moment nothing was further from her mind than London.

All she could think about was Oliver. The lazy, sexy look he was giving her from underneath thick, dark lashes, the way a tiny dimple appeared in the corner of his mouth when he smiled.

The way his mouth hovered tantalisingly close to hers.

Her breathing was shallow. He was so close that the temptation just to lift her mouth to his and finish what they'd started was enormous.

'I don't feel like a city girl any more.'

He gave a slow smile that was so unbelievably sexy that she felt her tummy tumble. 'Oh, dear,' he said softly, touching her cheek with his finger. 'In that case, it wouldn't be safe to let you go back to London. The big city is no place for a girl from the country.'

Helen chuckled but there was no escaping the fact that soon she would have to make a decision. She'd been given a month to drift. A month in which

Bryony had given her a home and Oliver had given her a job. But that month was up in another week.

And she needed to make a decision about what she was going to do with her life.

Tom dropped by the following morning while they were having breakfast to tell them that Lily had given birth to a little girl in the early hours of the morning.

'Tell me she was OK.' Oliver's expression was strained and Tom gave a long sigh.

'She was fine.' He yawned. 'I was there, wasn't I?'

'You didn't need to section her?'

Tom frowned. 'Why is everyone so obsessed with Caesarian sections these days? Believe it or not, women actually are designed to give birth, you know.' He helped himself to a mug from the cupboard and poured himself a coffee.

'So what happened?'

'You want a report on each contraction?'

Oliver rubbed a hand over the back of his neck and gave a wry smile. 'Am I that bad?'

'Yes.' Tom pulled out a chair and straddled it. 'But I forgive you because it's true that Lily was in a bad state, emotionally at least. She actually did have some damage from the previous delivery and it did cross my mind that I might have to section her, but she was so traumatised by the fact she felt so out of control last time that I decided to take a risk.'

'Her scar could have opened up.'

'In which case I would have repaired it,' Tom said calmly. 'As it is, Emma and I put her in the birthing pool, played her some music, kept her calm and she did it all by herself. Very relaxed. The sort of birth they have in the movies. You would have approved.'

Oliver looked at his brother. 'You stayed with her the whole time.'

'That was your request, I believe,' Tom drawled, leaning forward and helping himself to a piece of toast. 'I'll send you my bill.'

'How did you manage to not get called away? You always get called to handle the difficult stuff. Or wasn't there any difficult stuff?'

'There's always difficult stuff in obstetrics,' Tom said dryly. 'Babies insist on doing the unexpected instead of coming down the right route facing the right way. Last night I delegated. I happened to agree with you that Lily was important. And, actually, my registrar is showing a great deal of promise, which helps.'

'Well, thanks.' Oliver gave his brother a nod, his blue eyes warm. 'I'll buy you a drink tonight.'

'You will indeed.' Tom rose to his feet and reached for his jacket. 'I'm off. I just popped in to tell you about Lily.'

'What are you doing today?'

'Climbing. Ben and I are going together. Ellie has given him time off for good behaviour.'

Oliver grinned. 'Don't fall. I don't want to have to come out and rescue you.'

'Don't push your luck, bro.' Tom nodded to Helen in a friendly way and walked towards the door. 'By the way…' He turned back to Oliver, his eyes gleaming slightly. 'Isn't that roof of yours finished by now?'

Oliver smiled. 'It's coming along well,' he said softly. 'Very well indeed.'

'Glad to hear it because I'm sure I don't need to

remind you that Bryony and Jack are back next Saturday.' His eyes flicked to Helen and she smiled.

'I know. It's decision-making time. Find some-where to live or go back to London.'

Tom looked at her for a long moment. 'I'm sure you wouldn't have any trouble finding somewhere to live if you decide to stay.' He transferred his gaze to his brother. 'I'll see you tonight.'

He walked out and Oliver looked at Helen. 'The sun is shining, the sky is blue and there's snow on the ground. Fancy a walk?'

She nodded. 'It's been a busy week. I was hoping you'd suggest it.'

'Let's get going, then.'

They walked in companionable silence, their foot-steps muffled by the snow, the air still and calm.

When they finally stopped for a rest, their breath clouded the freezing air.

Oliver stared up at the sky with a frown. 'The weather is closing in. We should probably turn back soon.' He pulled a flask out of the rucksack and poured them both a drink. He handed a cup to Helen and then muttered under his breath as his mobile phone went off. 'Here…' He handed her his mug, too. 'Hold this for a sec, will you, please?'

While he answered the phone, Helen glanced up at the sky, too. When they'd started out they'd been able to see the tops of all the peaks. Now they were shrouded in mist.

Suddenly she gave a little shiver, relieved that she was with Oliver. It was frightening how quickly the weather could change in the mountains.

Oliver was talking on the phone, screwing up his

face slightly as he tried to decipher the crackle. 'You're not very clear.' He listened again and then nodded. 'That's better. OK, where is he?' There was another silence and then Oliver turned and glanced up the path. 'We're about half an hour from there.'

Helen felt herself tense. It was obviously a call from the mountain rescue centre. Was someone in trouble?

Oliver was still listening. 'We can be there faster than that. OK, send them, and I'll give you a call when we find him.'

He snapped the phone shut and retrieved his drink from Helen's fingers. Then he poured it carefully back into the flask, untouched.

'We might be needing this,' he muttered. 'A guy used his mobile phone to call the team. He was slurring his words and not making much sense. He wasn't that coherent and he couldn't be precise about his position, but Angie, who runs the bed and breakfast at the bottom of the valley, says he was seen heading up here first thing this morning. Apparently he's been staying with her for a few days on his own. He's in his fifties and overweight.'

'I hope he hasn't had a heart attack up here. He won't stand a chance, surely?' Helen quickly handed him her drink as well. 'I gather you want to try and find him yourself?'

Oliver let out a long breath. 'Well, they're sending the team out of course, but we're already halfway up his last known route so it seems sensible that we're the advance party. Do you mind? If he is where they think he should be then we can get to him quickly. In this weather time can make the difference between life and death. And I wouldn't do it if I thought there was any risk to you.'

He stroked a hand gently over her cheek and Helen felt her heart turn over.

She couldn't remember anyone ever making her feel so cared for.

She smiled. 'Of course we must go.' Even as she said the words, nerves fluttered in her stomach. She just hoped she didn't let him down.

She watched as he repacked his rucksack and lifted it onto his broad shoulders, trying not to think about the fact that the weather was closing in and fingers of cold were reaching inside her weatherproof jacket.

'That's my girl.' Oliver grinned and his eyes were warm with approval. 'Time to prove yourself, townie. We've been walking for the best part of three hours. It'll take a while for the rest of the team to assemble at base and then get themselves up here. So we're the advance party.'

Helen glanced at him. 'Just remember that I don't know anything about mountain rescue.'

'I'm the mountain rescue bit,' Oliver assured her firmly. 'You're my first-aid partner and general helper. If that man is having a heart attack in the mountains, I'm going to need your help.'

Helen peered doubtfully through the mist, wondering how steep the path became, and as if reading her mind Oliver reached into the rucksack and pulled out some gear.

'There is a bit of a drop up here,' he said honestly, 'but you won't be able to see it because of the mist. Just to make you feel safe, I'm going to clip a rope to you and attach it to myself. OK?'

More than OK.

Helen felt his strong hands fiddle with something at her waist and he jerked straps and adjusted buckles until he finally gave a grunt of satisfaction and clipped a rope to her.

This time Oliver walked with a sense of purpose, his pace steady as they climbed through the mist. Every now and then he stopped and checked their position and Helen stood still, not wanting to distract him and trying not to look over the edge. Because by now there was definitely an edge and she didn't want think about the drop.

'Footprints.' Oliver squatted down for a moment and then straightened. 'Could be his. On the other hand, it hasn't snowed for a couple of days so they could belong to someone else.'

His words were swallowed up by the roar of the waterfall that crashed down next to them and Helen winced as she felt the freezing spray on her face.

'It's really hard to make yourself heard here because of the noise of the waterfall,' Oliver shouted. 'It's virtually non-existent in summer but in the winter it powers down the mountain like a damn with a leak.' He broke off and his jaw tightened. 'Apparently, when he called, they could hear the falls in the background so he must be up this path somewhere if he took a direct route from the bed and breakfast.'

Helen squinted into the mist. 'Could he be the other side of the ghyll?'

Oliver shook his head. 'That's definitely not a tourist route. We'll carry on up here. My guess is we'll find him on this path. I reckon those are probably his footprints.'

But there was no sign of anyone and Oliver's loud

calls were virtually drowned by the sound of torrents of water thundering against the rocks.

His expression was grim and he glanced up the path. 'Come on, let's get going. We need to be a bit higher up.'

Higher up?

Helen took a deep breath and told herself that it wasn't possible to be afraid of heights if the mist was concealing the drop. That would be too stupid for words. She just needed to look at Oliver instead of the edge.

So she fixed her eyes on his broad shoulders and made a point of stepping where he stepped.

And then Oliver stopped dead, his gaze fixed on the snowy path.

Helen followed his line of vision. 'What's the matter?'

'Well, the footprints end here—the snow looks crushed. As if someone fell.' He bent down and touched it with his glove, a frown on his handsome face. 'And some of the snow has been knocked off the edge…'

Realising what he was suggesting, Helen stared at him in horror. 'You think he fell?'

'He was certainly alive when he made the call.' Oliver straightened up, pulled her back away from the edge and unclipped her rope.

'Stand there and don't move,' he said firmly. 'You'll be fine. I just want to see if I can spot him. He may not be there at all, of course, but I have this feeling—'

He removed his rucksack and Helen watched while he pulled out a rope and various other bits and pieces that she couldn't identify.

Then he walked towards the edge and shouted something.

Helen strained her ears to see if she could hear a reply but the roar of the water was almost deafening.

Oliver suddenly vanished from sight and Helen felt her heart lurch. Without his reassuring presence the mountains suddenly seemed less welcoming. She glanced around her but the mist created an unnerving stillness that made her shiver.

She looked hopefully towards the edge again but there was no sign of Oliver.

There was no point in shouting because she knew he couldn't hear her so she stayed where she was for a few more minutes and then gingerly inched towards the edge.

Telling herself that he might need her help, Helen forced herself forwards until she could peer into the ghyll. The mist prevented her from seeing very far and the roar of the water was almost deafening. Huge rocks loomed into her vision, shiny from the spray of water and interspersed with patches of frozen snow. And finally she saw Oliver below her, balanced on a rock, holding onto the body of a man.

At first Helen thought the man must be unconscious but then she saw him move and felt a flood of relief.

At least they weren't dealing with a body.

She watched in horror as Oliver dragged the slumped figure as far away from the edge as possible, his face damp from the spray of the water.

She closed her eyes briefly, forcing herself to face the inevitable. It was perfectly obvious that he needed help and the only help available was her. Which meant going down the rock to him.

Could she do that?

She stared down at the glistening surface and decided that there seemed to be quite a few handholds.

Without allowing time for her fright to grow any further, she took a deep breath and turned around, lowering herself gingerly over the rock. At least it was misty so she couldn't see the extent of the drop.

Trying to ignore the biting cold, she moved slowly, lowering herself carefully, only moving a hand when she was sure that both feet were firmly placed on something solid. Once she slipped and her insides dropped with fear until she felt her feet once more rest safely on the rock.

Her heart still pounding ridiculously fast, she risked a hesitant glance downwards and for a brief moment the mist cleared, showing her the steep, vertiginous drop to the bottom.

Oh, dear God…

Her vision blurred and she closed her eyes immediately, clinging to the rock as panic swamped her usually rational brain.

'It's all right, angel, I've got you.' Oliver's voice, firm and masculine, came from right underneath her. The next moment he was next to her, one strong arm fastened firmly around her waist, securing her to the rock. 'I've got you, sweetheart. You're not going to fall. Take a few deep breaths and don't look down.'

He felt solid and safe and Helen felt herself relax slightly.

Then she remembered what was below her.

'I know I'm being pathetic, but I don't think I can move, Oliver,' she said shakily, hating herself for being so useless but horribly aware of the vicious drop that lay below them.

'I don't want you to move until I tell you to.'

She felt his hand at her waist. Felt him clip a rope onto her harness. But mostly she felt him, warm and amazingly reassuring right behind her. He was like a safety blanket between her and terror.

'Good girl. You've been very brave,' he murmured in her ear. 'And I'm glad you did it because I need your help. This man needs your help. You're almost down, Helen. Just a few more steps and you're there.'

Her eyes were still tightly shut. 'I can't do it—I'm going to fall.'

'You're not going to fall. You're attached to me and I have no intention of going anywhere.' He gave her shoulder a final squeeze and then moved his arm. 'I'm going to go first, and then I'm going to tell you where to put your hands and feet. Just do exactly what I say.'

He did just that and she climbed down the rest of the way like a robot, following his instructions, taking his hand whenever he offered it.

And finally she was safe.

If standing on an exposed rock, facing a furious waterfall could be described as safe.

Trying not to think about it, Helen gradually released her grip on Oliver's hand.

'OK—brilliant. Now, don't go near the edge because it's slippery.'

Helen managed a smile. 'Oliver, you don't need to tell me not to go near the edge,' she said and he grinned in return.

'Maybe I don't. In that case, let's see what we can do to help this chap. I've told the team where we are. Some of them should be here pretty shortly. He's conscious but only just. I haven't had a chance to have a proper look at him yet.'

The man was slumped against the rock, his eyes glazed. He tried to say something but his words slurred together. He gave a groan and his eyes drifted shut.

'Apparently his name is Brian Andrews. Can you hear me, Mr Andrews?' Oliver tried to rouse the man who opened his eyes with what seemed to be a supreme effort. 'Brian? I'm a doctor. Can you talk to me? Are you in pain?'

The man mumbled something incomprehensible and knocked Oliver's hand away when he tried to take his pulse.

'Whoa. Calm down—we're here to help you.' Oliver backed off slightly and Helen dropped to her knees beside him, anxious to help.

'Do you have any pain, Mr Andrews?' Her voice was soft and gentle and the man turned his head towards her, his eyes glazed as he tried to focus.

'Need to go home.' He swung his arms wildly and tried to get up, but Oliver restrained him.

'You need to keep as still ask you can for a moment,' he advised. 'There's a steep drop down there.'

The man swung his arms again and Helen looked at Oliver in confusion.

'Why is he behaving like this when we're trying to help him?' she asked, her eyes swivelling back to the man. 'He's very pale and sweaty.'

'Yeah. I need to examine him.'

But it didn't look as though that was going to be a possibility. The man snarled at them aggressively and suddenly he reminded Helen of a patient she'd once treated.

She gave a soft gasp. 'Oliver, do we have any hot chocolate left in that flask?'

'Yes.' His eyes lifted to hers as he interpreted the reason for her question. 'You think he's diabetic?'

'I don't know. But his symptoms remind me of a patient I nursed once. Everyone thought he was drunk but he was hypoglycaemic. He was slurring his words like this and he was sweaty and pale. And I seem to remember that he was also pretty irritable.'

Oliver took another look at the man and gave a short laugh. 'Well, it's certainly worth a try.' Rocking back on his heels, he delved into the rucksack and pulled out the flask. 'I hope you're right. See if you can find some sort of SOS bracelet or any medication on him.'

Helen leaned forward, her voice gentle. 'Are you a diabetic, Mr Andrews?' She spoke soothingly to the man, her fingers rolling back the sleeves of his jacket as she searched for clues. This time the man lay unresisting. 'No bracelet, no chain, nothing. But his pulse is very fast. I'm sure he's a diabetic, Oliver.'

Oliver nodded. 'I'm beginning to agree with you and we're definitely going to give it a try. There's not much else we can do until the team arrives anyway. We can't get him off this rock by ourselves. All right, give me a hand to hold him while I get him to drink this. We're lucky. Any longer and he wouldn't have been in a state to eat anything, and I'm not in the habit of carrying injectable glucose when I go for a walk.'

They propped the man in a sitting position and then Oliver poured a small amount of their hot chocolate into a plastic mug.

'Make sure it isn't too hot,' Helen warned anxiously, and Oliver tested the liquid quickly.

'It's fine. It's not going to burn anyone. Just very

sweet, which is exactly what he needs if his problem is what you think it is. He needs fast-acting oral carbohydrate.'

Helen bit her lip, her heart thudding hard against her chest. She hoped desperately that she was right.

But surely, if he was a diabetic, the man would have been wearing a bracelet?

'Can you drink this for me?' Oliver murmured, pressing the cup to the man's lips and encouraging him to take sips. 'That's great. And more if you can. That's it. I think this is going to help.'

Oliver persisted until the mug was empty and then turned to Helen. 'There's some chocolate in the front pocket of my rucksack. Let's give him that, too.'

It was a slow process but gradually the man cooperated and ate the chocolate and his condition started to improve markedly.

Fifteen minutes after they'd given him the hot chocolate he was able to talk clearly. 'Thanks.' He wiped a shaking hand across his mouth. 'I seem to have got myself in a spot of trouble…'

Helen shot Oliver an incredulous glance. As understatements went, it was impressive. The man had been incredibly lucky. Had they not been in the area he might have died before help had arrived.

'You're a diabetic,' Helen said gently, 'but I couldn't find a bracelet or anything to tell us that.'

The man's eyes drifted shut and he let out a long breath. 'Don't want to be labelled,' he muttered, shaking his head slightly. 'Don't want it to interfere with my life. Just want to get on and do the things I've always done.'

'Right.' Oliver ran a hand over the back of his neck. 'Well, you can do most of the things you've always done, providing you control your blood sugar properly. You've just done a fairly strenuous walk. Did you bring food with you?'

The man shook his head. 'Didn't plan to be out that long.'

'You were suffering from something called hypoglycaemia,' Oliver explained, 'which basically means that your blood sugar was dangerously low. It usually happens when you take more exercise than you were planning or when you delay a meal. Or sometimes if you give yourself too much insulin. Presumably you attend a diabetic clinic?'

The man gave a grunt. 'Load of bloody busybodies—always telling you what to do and checking up on you.'

'They're trying to help you control your diabetes,' Helen said gently, giving his hand a squeeze, but he brushed her hand away.

'I can control it by myself.'

Helen opened her mouth to speak but Oliver caught her eye and gave a discreet shake of his head.

'All right.' His voice was calm and even. 'Well, you're clearly feeling better in yourself but you had quite a fall. You obviously lost your balance on the path and managed to tumble down here. It's amazing that you didn't fall all the way to the bottom. Are you hurting anywhere?'

The man struggled to his feet, brushing away all offers of help. 'No. I'm fine. I just went for a stroll and I started to feel dizzy.'

At that moment there was a shout from above and Sean Nicholson, the A and E consultant, abseiled quickly down a rope, landing neatly next to them.

Helen stared at him in awe, remembering how long it had taken her to climb down that same route.

'I've never seen anyone do that before.' She smiled at him in admiration. 'I must say it looked a great deal more entertaining than clinging to slippery rocks with fingernails, which was my experience.'

Oliver winked and took some equipment from Sean. 'Hell on the nail varnish, don't you find, Sean?'

'Nightmare. That's why I chose the easy route. Good afternoon, Mr Andrews.' Sean gave the patient a friendly nod, listening while Oliver related what had happened.

'If you're going to nag me, then please don't bother,' the man said grumpily and Sean frowned slightly.

'My job is just to get you down safely from this mountain,' he said smoothly. 'And to recommend that you get yourself checked out at the hospital before you carry on with your holiday.' He glanced at Helen and then looked at Oliver. 'You two should probably make a move. Helen's looking cold. We can manage here easily enough now. You've done the hard bit.'

And Helen realised that she was actually freezing.

Sitting still on that rock, the chill had suddenly penetrated her bones and she started to shiver.

'Oliver...' A disturbing thought had struck her and she glanced upwards, a horrified expression on her face. 'Am I going to have to climb back up the way I came down?'

'No. From this point it's quicker to carry on to the bottom,' Sean said immediately. 'You turn right and meet up with the path. Oliver knows the way.'

'Down?'

Remembering the drop, she glanced at them in horror.

'Sean's right,' Oliver said quickly, fastening his rucksack and swinging it onto his back. 'It isn't far from here. You've done the worst bit.'

Without giving her time to brood, he clipped a rope to her waist, gave her harness a tug and guided her towards the edge of the rocks.

The sound of the waterfall was so loud they could hardly make themselves heard and Oliver glanced back at Sean who was coordinating with the rest of the team.

'Drunken Fox, tonight?'

Sean grinned. 'You're buying.'

Oliver went first and then guided Helen down until finally they reached the bottom and picked up the path.

'How long will it take them to get him off the mountain?' Helen asked, tugging her hood up to protect her head from the steadily falling snow. 'Will they be all right?'

Oliver glanced at her in amusement. 'They'll be fine. And it shouldn't take them long. Couple of hours?'

'And then what?' Helen frowned as she huddled deeper inside her coat. 'He's obviously determined to ignore his disease. Will they try and persuade him to take it more seriously?'

'Helen, we're the mountain rescue team,' Oliver reminded her gently. 'We rescue people from mountains. It's not our job to sort out the rest of their lives, however much we might like to. Sean will try and persuade him to go to hospital to be checked and he'll certainly tell him that he needs to see his GP, but after that it's out of our hands.'

'Well, it was a very exciting walk. And I must admit I was shocked by how quickly the mist came down,' Helen said with a shudder. 'One minute we had virtually blue skies, the next we could barely see. But that might have been a good thing, I suppose. If I'd been able to see all the way to the bottom of that ghyll I never would have plucked up the courage to climb over those rocks.'

They reached the car and Oliver shrugged the rucksack off his back.

'You were great. I would never have known you were born and bred in the city.'

Helen stood still, her eyes on the mountains that she was steadily growing to love. 'It's going to be really hard to leave.'

Oliver heaved his rucksack into the boot, slammed it shut and turned to face her. 'Then don't.' His voice was hoarse. 'Don't leave, Helen. Stay.'

He cupped her face in his hands and lowered his mouth to hers, his kiss so hot and urgent that she felt flames reach up from deep within and devour her self-control.

She felt the erotic lick of his tongue, felt his strong hands drawing her against him, felt the flash of energy and passion that exploded between them.

With the temperature dropping rapidly, she should have felt cold, but all she felt was warmth.

When he finally eased away from her, she felt bereft and looked at him in disbelief and confusion.

How could he bring an end to something so perfect?

'It will be dark soon. We need to get home.'

Helen hid her disappointment, uncomfortably aware that she wouldn't have been able to end that kiss even if an avalanche had engulfed them both.

'Right…' She tried to look suitably indifferent. As if kisses like that came and went all the time.

He gave a humourless laugh and ran a hand over the back of her neck. 'If you're for one moment thinking that I found it easy to stop that kiss, there's something I ought to tell you.' He curved a hand under her chin and forced her to look at him. 'Next time I kiss you, townie, I'm not stopping.'

CHAPTER EIGHT

THE Drunken Fox was crowded with people that evening, but for Helen there was only Oliver.

She couldn't remember ever being so aware of a man.

They'd finished their walk in virtual silence and when they'd arrived back at the cottage, Oliver had pushed her gently towards the stairs.

'You have the first shower,' he'd said gruffly. 'We're going out in less than an hour.'

And now they were both in the pub and all Helen could think about was going home again.

Realising that in just a few hours they would be alone in the cottage together with no threat of interruptions, Helen felt her tummy tumble with a mixture of nerves and anticipation.

Oliver had made it perfectly clear that he wanted their relationship to go all the way.

Did she?

From the moment they'd entered the pub, Oliver hadn't strayed from her side, and even now she could feel the brush of his muscular shoulder against hers as he lounged casually against the bar, chatting to Tom.

It came as no surprise that he seemed to know everyone in the pub, and after three weeks in the Lake District Helen was starting to get used to the fact that everyone seemed to know everyone else's business.

And she liked it. Liked the fact that people cared about each other.

She glanced around the cosy pub, loving the warm, intimate atmosphere created by a flickering log fire and a bunch of people who clearly knew each other extremely well. It smelt of wood smoke and welcome, a place to relax after a hard day.

She felt Oliver's arm slide around her waist, trapping her against him as he stood chatting to his brother at the bar.

He was wearing a pair of worn jeans that moulded themselves perfectly to the hard muscle of his thighs and a soft wool jumper that emphasised the breadth and power of his shoulders.

He looked so sexy and male that she was finding it hard to breathe.

And he seemed so relaxed it was hard to believe that he was the same man who'd kissed her breathless earlier.

Perhaps he'd changed his mind about the way he felt.

And then he turned to say something to her and something in his gaze made her realise that he wasn't relaxed at all. And he certainly hadn't changed his mind.

He was biding his time.

So it came as no surprise when he finally looked at his watch and reached for his jacket.

'Time to go home,' he said easily, taking her hand and nodding to his brother. 'See you tomorrow.'

Still holding her hand tightly, he led her out of the pub and they walked to his car.

They drove home in silence and by the time he

finally pulled up outside Bryony's cottage, the tension between them had reached an almost intolerable level.

Oliver switched off the engine and stared into the darkness for a moment.

Then he turned and his eyes burned into hers. 'Helen, we both know what's going to happen once we walk inside that door so if this isn't what you want…'

Delicious, forbidden excitement squirmed low in her stomach and suddenly she found the answer she'd been searching for. 'It's what I want.'

She didn't understand why, but Helen had moved beyond trying to understand what it was that she felt for Oliver.

'Then let's go inside.'

He unlocked the door of the cottage but instead of putting on the lights he walked straight through to the cosy living room.

'Oliver?' She followed him through, stopping in the doorway as she realised that the room was full of candles. And Oliver already had half of them alight.

He must have set them up before they left for the evening and she hadn't even noticed.

The flickering light gave a seductive, mysterious glow and Helen watched as he lit the log fire.

She was still wearing her coat and he crossed the room towards her and slid it from her shoulders, his eyes holding hers.

'I happen to love this room, but if you're cold then we can go upstairs…'

'I'm not cold.'

'You're shivering.'

'That's not because I'm cold.' She closed her eyes, aware that his clever fingers were making short work of the tiny buttons on her cardigan.

'So why are you shivering?' His voice was low and husky and she felt the seductive brush of his fingers against her flesh and suddenly she was standing there in only her lacy bra and her jeans. 'Why, Helen?'

She swallowed, her heart pounding as she stared up at him. 'Because I want you. But I'm scared, Oliver.'

His hands stilled. 'Scared?'

'Scared of hurting you.' Her voice was a whisper. 'I don't know what I want. I don't—'

'Shh…' He covered her lips with a gentle finger. 'No more talking.'

And just to make doubly sure that she couldn't talk, he lowered his mouth to hers.

And his kiss snapped the last of her feeble resistance.

Stifled by sexual anticipation, her heart thudding out of control, Helen lifted her hands to his jumper and instantly he took over, dragging his mouth away from hers and stripping himself naked to the waist.

Her pulse rocketed and her breathing stopped. For the past few weeks she seemed to have become more and more aware of Oliver's body but even those increasingly frequent glances hadn't prepared her for the reality. And she hadn't known it was possible to want a man with such fierce desperation.

Her eyes slid down his muscular chest, following the line of curling dark hairs that trailed downwards and vanished under the waistband of his jeans. And then her gaze slid lower still to the very visible evidence of his erection straining against the unforgiving fabric.

'See what you do to me?' He slid a strong hand behind her head, sliding his fingers into the softness of her hair and holding her firmly. 'You've been do-ing that to me since the first moment I saw you.'

Without giving her a chance to reply, he guided her head towards him and met her halfway, his mouth descending on hers with hot, restless purpose.

Wild, intoxicating excitement exploded inside her and she kissed him back, exchanging bite for bite and lick for lick. He tortured with his mouth and teased with his hands until she realised that somehow they were both naked.

Without stopping to wonder how he'd accom-plished that without her noticing, Helen pressed closer to him, shivering at the first touch of his flesh against hers.

She felt warmth and heat and pounding excitement and then he scooped her off her feet and carried her to the rug in front of the fire.

He lowered her gently and then came down on top of her and she sobbed with pleasure as she felt the solid weight of his body on hers, felt his skilled, clever fingers seeking the burning heat of her femi-ninity.

He muttered something into her hair and then slid down her quivering, writhing body and fastened his mouth on her breast. The skilled flick of his tongue over her already hardened nipple made her gasp and arch against him and she dug her nails into the hard muscle of his shoulders, tortured by sensation.

His fingers explored her intimately but it wasn't enough and she sobbed his name in a plea for more.

He lifted his head, his gaze burning into hers. 'What?'

'Please, Oliver...' Her voice sounded broken and

she slid one hand down his body and closed her slender fingers over his pulsing arousal. 'Please, now...'

His gaze darkened and his breathing became harsh and rapid as he slid an arm under hips. 'Look at me Helen, I want you to look at me.'

Didn't he know that she wasn't capable of anything else? At that precise moment she wanted to spend the rest of her life drowning in Oliver's blue gaze, feeling the heat of his body on hers.

With a flicker of delicious anticipation she felt the hard throb of his erection touching her intimately and then he entered her with a powerful thrust, driven by the almost intolerable need that consumed both of them.

Her vision blurred and she shuddered as she felt him thrust again, felt his strength and power deep within her. Her muscles tensed and then rippled, drawing him in.

'Don't move,' he pleaded hoarsely, his breathing fractured as he struggled for control. 'Just stay still for a minute.'

But she couldn't stay still. She shifted under him, rotating her hips, and he groaned and thrust deep in response to her provocative movements, losing the battle he'd been fighting for control.

And still their gazes held. Held as they moved together, held as their flesh grew slick and damp and held as he drove them both to a climax so intense and all-consuming that Helen forgot about everything except Oliver.

For a single, breathless moment in time she belonged to him.

She was part of him.

And finally he closed his eyes and buried his face in her hair.

'I love you, Helen.'

His soft words brought a gasp to her throat and tears to her eyes. She opened her mouth to say the words back to him but no sound emerged.

It had felt so special but she couldn't work out why.

What was the magic ingredient? Why had it felt so different?

'Oliver…'

He lifted his head and kissed her gently, a wry smile of understanding in his blue eyes. 'It's all right—I know it's all too soon for you.'

So why was she lying underneath him feeling as though she never, ever wanted to move?

Helen nursed a cup of coffee and stared out of the kitchen window towards the mountains, wondering how everything in her life could have changed so much in just three weeks.

Her aching body was a delicious reminder of the night before and she ran a hand from her waist to her hips, as if aware of herself for the first time.

I love you.

She closed her eyes briefly, reliving the moment when he'd said those words with a thrill of excitement.

And then she remembered David.

David had said those words, too. Just before he'd caught a plane to Singapore with another woman.

Words were, after all, just words. Anyone could say them. Especially when sharing the intimacies that she and Oliver had the night before.

If David hadn't meant those words after six years, how could she expect Oliver to after only three weeks? No one fell in love in three weeks. It wasn't possible. Love needed time to grow.

She was still brooding when there was a loud knock on the door.

Assuming it would be Tom, Helen put down her coffee and walked quickly to the door, opening it with a smile on her face.

David stood there.

Helen's smile faded and emotion rushed through her with the force of a tornado.

Something must have shown on her face because he gave a slight grimace and ran a hand through his hair. 'If you're going to hit me, perhaps you'd better do it now and get it over with. But at least let me talk. I've been driving all night.'

Noticing that he was wearing a thin suit and footwear totally unsuitable for the weather, Helen stood to one side.

It didn't occur to her that three weeks previously she wouldn't have noticed such a thing.

'You'd better come in before you freeze.' Her voice was strangely flat. Five weeks ago all she'd wanted had been the opportunity to talk to David. To find out why he'd done what he had. Now she couldn't remember what it was she'd wanted to say to him.

He walked past her into the cottage and paused in the hallway. 'Helen…'

'Let's go into the kitchen,' she said quickly, glancing anxiously towards the stairs. For some reason it seemed extremely important that Oliver didn't come downstairs yet. At some point during the night the fire had gone out and they'd moved to the bedroom.

And Oliver was still asleep...

David frowned slightly but shrugged and followed her through to the kitchen, his expression wary as she turned to face him.

'I'm going to come straight to the point.' He gave her that lopsided smile that she'd once found so attractive. 'I made a mistake, Helen. A huge mistake. And I admit it. We never should have split up.'

Helen stirred. '*We* didn't split up,' she said politely. 'You left me at the altar.'

Bright spots of colour appeared on his cheekbones and he shifted his weight uncomfortably. 'Well, not exactly. I—'

'I hadn't actually arrived at the church,' Helen agreed helpfully, 'but it was a close thing.'

David gave a sigh and ran a hand over his face. 'Look—you have every right to be angry. But we were together for six years. Is that really something that you can throw away lightly?'

'You did,' Helen pointed out calmly, and David frowned.

'What's wrong with you? You've changed,' he said quietly. 'You never used to answer back or be confrontational.'

'Well, maybe you just didn't know me, David.'

'Listen, sweetie.' He spread his hands in a gesture of apology. 'Everyone makes a mistake at some point in their lives. Well, this was mine. And now I'm going to put it right. I want you back.'

He wanted her back?

Helen stared at him, waiting to feel a rush of relief

and pleasure. Waiting for the impulse to throw her arms around him.

Nothing happened.

Her eyes slid over him, noting his perfectly groomed appearance. Despite the fact he claimed to have driven all night, there was no trace of stubble on his freshly shaved jaw. He looked as though he'd just stepped out of the courtroom—his tie neatly adjusted, the flash designer watch gleaming on his wrist.

He looked rich, sophisticated and self-confident. Most women's idea of a perfect partner. And he wanted her back.

It seemed that shattered dreams could be glued together again after all.

She looked at him, searching her brain and her heart for the answer.

However much he'd hurt her, they had been together for six years.

She'd been expecting to exchange vows with this man.

She could still have the life she'd mapped out for herself.

Oliver woke to find the other half of the bed empty.

He rolled over, his body reacting instantly to the subtle scent of Helen's perfume still clinging to her pillow.

Where was she?

They'd made love all night, so ravenous for each other that they hadn't broken contact until the light had started to intrude through the curtains. They'd savoured and lingered and feasted on each other until, clinging together in blissful, satiated exhaustion, they'd finally fallen asleep.

And for the first time in his life he'd laid himself bare emotionally. Stripped himself naked in every sense, willing to trust this precious woman with his heart.

For the first time in his life, he'd said *I love you.*

He covered his eyes with his forearm and cursed softly, grimly aware that despite the unbelievable physical intimacies they'd shared, Helen hadn't once said those words back to him.

But, then, Helen didn't think that love could happen so quickly.

Or did she still think that she was in love with David?

Deciding that he'd given her enough space, Oliver pulled on jeans and a jumper and padded downstairs, pausing on the bottom step as he heard Helen's voice coming from the kitchen.

He frowned.

He hadn't heard the door.

'I'm really glad you came, David,' she was saying and Oliver froze.

David? *She was talking to David?*

And she was glad he'd come?

Unprepared for the pain that seared his chest, Oliver pushed open the door of his sister's kitchen and saw Helen wrapped in a man's arms.

David's arms.

'Excuse me.' If he'd had his way he wouldn't even have announced himself, but to make his escape he needed his jacket and his car keys and both were in the kitchen.

He cast one long look over the man who had once been Helen's fiancé and who was obviously destined to hold that position again. If he hadn't heard those words himself—*I'm really glad you came, David*—he would have flattened the guy for the way he'd treated Helen.

But clearly such heroics were uncalled for.

So instead he walked calmly into the kitchen, trying not to notice that Helen was still in her dressing-gown. The thought that she was still naked under there filled him with almost unbearable tension.

Last night she'd been his.

Every warm, feminine inch of her.

'Oliver…' Helen pulled away from David and turned towards him, clearly embarrassed and Oliver managed a smile. In fact, he was fairly proud of the smile. Considering the way he was feeling, it was a hell of a convincing smile.

But he didn't want Helen feeling guilty.

He knew better than anyone how confused she'd felt over David and if she wanted him back in her life he certainly wasn't going to stand in her way.

'I need to go to the surgery.'

'But you're not working.'

He gave a shrug and reached for his keys and his coat. 'You know me by now, Helen. I'm always working.'

And he no longer had a reason to stay.

Helen stared after Oliver and suddenly everything was clear.

Like the mist lifting from the mountains, she suddenly saw what she wanted her future to be with perfect clarity.

But was it too late?

Was Oliver just going to walk away from what they'd shared the night before?

She stood frozen to the spot and then the heavy slam of the front door galvanised her into action and she sprinted after him, desperate to talk to him, totally oblivious of the fact that David was still standing in the kitchen.

She tugged open the front door, frantic to get to Oliver, but Oliver put his foot down, scattering shingle and snow as he drove away at speed.

'No!' Feeling utterly desolate, Helen's slim shoulders slumped and she stared after him helplessly. Then she noticed the four-wheel drive.

He'd taken the sex machine. Which meant she could go after him.

Lost in thought, she gave a start as she felt a hand on her shoulder.

She'd totally forgotten about David.

He stared after Oliver's car with disapproval. 'Who was that? He was driving far too fast for the road conditions.'

'That,' she said quietly, 'is the man I love. And he's used to the road conditions. He's lived here all his life.'

She turned, noticing how ridiculous David looked in his expensive suit. She'd always thought he was good-looking but suddenly she found herself noticing that his shoulders weren't as broad as Oliver's and he didn't smile with his eyes. In fact, no matter which way you looked at it, he just wasn't Oliver.

She tried to imagine David climbing into a ditch to save a woman's life or making a call on a Sunday unless he was being paid an exorbitant hourly rate.

She tried to imagine David making love to her the way Oliver had the night before.

Her face heated at the memory and she gave a soft smile.

Love.

That was the secret ingredient.

That was the reason it had felt different.

'Are you seriously suggesting that you love that man? You can't possibly love him.' David looked at her in bemusement. 'You can't have known the guy for more than a few weeks.'

'But time doesn't have anything to do with it, does it David?' she said quietly, suddenly desperate to go after Oliver and talk to him. 'You and I were together for six years, but I don't think you ever knew the real me. And I don't think I knew you either.'

David looked thoroughly out of his depth. 'Shall we continue this conversation indoors?' he suggested, glancing up at the sky with a frown. 'It's freezing out here.'

Helen shook her head. 'Actually, I like it out here. The air is really clean and there isn't anything more to be said. I'm really glad you came, David, because it helped me realise that we are not a good match.'

'That's ridiculous.' David looked at her. 'You would have made a perfect lawyer's wife.'

'No.' Helen lifted her chin. 'I'm me, David. I'm not here to make your life easier. If that's what you want, find yourself a secretary. And now I need to get dressed.'

And with that she hurried back into the cottage and up the stairs.

She needed to see Oliver.

She found him in the surgery, absorbed by something on the computer.

'Oliver?'

He lifted his head, his expression distant. 'Hi, there.'

She remembered just how close they'd been the night before, how he'd held her and made love to her, and wondered how he could be so reserved.

Her heart plummeted.

That cool reserve hurt her more than she could possibly have imagined.

Had she misread the situation?

'Listen, about David—'

'It doesn't matter, Helen.' His tone was steady and he turned his attention back to the computer. 'You must be thrilled that he came back.'

She looked for signs of jealousy. Anything that suggested that he minded, but there was nothing.

Misery spread through her.

If he didn't mind that David had come back, that could only mean one thing.

'Oliver—'

'Our relationship probably helped you put your feelings for him in perspective. It was just a bit of fun. I hope you're not feeling guilty about it.'

Helen stared at him, really shocked by his almost indifferent response.

Last night he'd kissed every inch of her quivering body.

Last night they'd whispered intimacies and shared secrets.

Last night he'd told her that he loved her.

And now he was talking to her as though she were a patient.

'Tell me honestly…' Her voice was croaky and

suddenly she found that her hands were shaking. 'Do you regret last night?'

There was a long silence and when he finally turned to face her she noticed the lines of tiredness around his kind blue eyes. 'Yes,' he said quietly, 'I suppose I do.'

Pain stifled her breathing and she backed away from him. She'd heard all she needed to hear.

'I'm sorry.' Her voice was barely audible and she grabbed the door handle for support. 'If it's any consolation it won't matter because I've decided to go back to London. I'm catching the train tonight. You won't have to see me again.'

He gave a brief nod, not in the slightest surprised, and Helen was astonished by the depth of her own disappointment.

What had she expected?

That he'd try and stop her? That he'd beg her to stay?

He'd already told her that he regretted their relationship.

There was nothing left to say except goodbye.

But the words stuck in her throat and Oliver seemed more interested in his computer than her.

So Helen quietly put his car keys on his desk, slid out of the room and walked out of the surgery with tears in her eyes.

She'd get a taxi back to the cottage, pick up her bags and go to the station before Bryony and Jack arrived home. That way she wouldn't be a wet blanket.

She stood for a moment in the car park, staring at

the mountains, thinking that in a month she'd recovered from David.

All she had to do now was recover from Oliver.

But she knew that what she felt for Oliver would be with her forever.

CHAPTER NINE

OLIVER stared blindly at the monitor, fighting the temptation to put his fist through it.

It had taken every ounce of will-power on his part not to crash his way through his desk and grab Helen.

But the image of her in David's arms had stayed with him.

He tried to console himself with the fact that four weeks ago his life had been happy.

Four weeks ago his life had been fine.

But that had been before he'd met Helen.

The door to his consulting room flew open and he glanced up eagerly, his broad shoulders sagging slightly when he saw his brother standing there.

'What's wrong?'

Tom strolled into the room, pushing the door shut behind him. 'Bryony just rang from the airport. She's on her way back. I came to warn you so that you can rethink accommodation for you and Helen.'

'Thanks, but it's all sorted. I'm going home after I've finished here.'

'Home to your home?' Tom lifted an eyebrow mockingly. 'And what about your roof?'

Oliver didn't smile. 'My roof is finished.'

Tom looked at him searchingly. 'And Helen?'

There was a long silence and when Oliver finally spoke his voice sounded rusty. 'David has turned up.'

'David? The guy who left her?'

'The same.'

'And she slapped his face, yes?'

'Not when I was there,' Oliver said evenly. 'In fact, they were looking pretty cosy. She came here to say goodbye. She's on her way back to London, presumably to begin the life she had planned before he ditched her at the altar. He's about to make her a very happy woman.'

'Are you sure about that?' Tom frowned. 'I just saw her climbing into a taxi, looking as though her best friend had died. She certainly didn't look like a woman who'd rediscovered the love of her life.'

Oliver gave a twisted smile. 'Helen's a sweet girl. I expect she was worrying that she'd hurt me. I tried to pretend that it was all just a bit of fun and that none of it mattered, but I don't think I was very convincing.'

Tom looked at him, his eyes searching. 'And you're sure you didn't misunderstand?'

'I heard her say that she was glad to see him,' Oliver muttered, running a hand over his face and slumping in his chair. 'Damn, Tom. I never thought it would hurt this much.'

'Love?' Tom gave a harsh laugh. 'Love is the worst pain known to man.'

Momentarily distracted, Oliver looked at his brother, realising that the statement had deeper implications. 'I assume you're talking about Sally. I've always wanted to know why you ended it.'

'Because I thought she was too young to make that sort of commitment…' Tom paused for a moment and his firm mouth curved into a smile of self-mockery. 'And I was stupid,' he finished softly. 'Incredibly stupid.'

Knowing that Tom never talked about Sally, Oliver

held his breath. 'And if you could put the clock back?'

'It's too late for that,' Tom said harshly, glancing quickly at his watch, 'but it isn't too late for you. I suggest you go back to the cottage and knock him down. Then drag the maiden back to your lair and have your wicked way with her.'

He'd done that the night before.

It didn't seem to have made even the slightest difference to her final decision.

Oliver gave a weary smile. 'Helen's made her choice.'

Tom frowned. 'That doesn't sound like you. If you love her, fight for her! You've always fought for everything you believed in. Literally, when you were younger. You had permanent black eyes at one point.'

Oliver shook his head. 'The one thing I can't fight is her love for another man, Tom. It has to be her decision. And she's made it.'

Helen stood on the freezing platform, wishing the train would arrive.

Once she was safely on her way, maybe she'd lose the desperate urge to run back to Oliver.

She glanced around her, realising that she was the only person waiting for the train.

Five more minutes. Five more minutes and then the Lake District would be part of her past.

And so would Oliver.

From the tiny station car park she heard the slam of a car door, a masculine shout and then footsteps. Her heart lifted, only to plummet again as she saw Tom striding towards her.

'Is something wrong?' She looked around her but

the platform was still empty, which meant that she could be the only reason for the visit.

'Plenty.' Tom raked long fingers through his dark hair. 'Look, I'm probably going to say the wrong thing here—heaven knows, I've made a complete mess of my own love life so I'm certainly not qualified to tamper with anyone else's—' He broke off and took a deep breath. 'Do you love Oliver?'

Helen looked at him, startled. 'Sorry?'

Tom gritted his teeth impatiently. 'Do you love my brother?'

'Well, I—'

'It's a simple question, Helen. Yes or no?'

'Yes,' she croaked, rubbing the toe of her boot on the frosty surface of the platform. 'Yes, I do. But it was just a bit of fun for him.'

Tom gave a disbelieving laugh. 'You may love him, but you don't know him very well, do you? He thinks you're reunited with David. He doesn't want you to feel guilty about going back to him. He's making things easy for you. It's pure Oliver.'

'Easy?' Helen stared at him and swallowed hard. 'Seeing Oliver so cool this morning was the hardest thing I've ever had to bear, particularly after last night—' She broke off and blushed, realising what she'd just said, but Tom gripped her shoulders, forcing her to look at him.

'So you're not going back to David?'

She shook her head. 'No. I couldn't. I love Oliver.'

'Then why are you going back to London?'

Helen glanced down the track and saw the train approaching. 'Because I can't live here and see Oliver every day. It would hurt too much, knowing that he doesn't love me.'

'He does love you.' Tom swore under his breath and stared at the approaching train with something close to desperation. 'No wonder the path of true love never runs smoothly,' he muttered. 'People don't tell each other the truth.'

'Oliver has only known me for three weeks.'

'Oliver loved you from the first moment he saw you,' Tom said. 'He moved into Bryony's cottage, for goodness' sake, just so that he could be with you because he couldn't bring himself to leave you on your own.'

Helen frowned, suddenly confused. 'He was having his roof done.'

Tom sighed. 'Helen, Oliver's roof is fine. Rock solid. Not a leak in sight.'

Helen stared at him. 'But—'

'He was determined to watch over you. Pure Oliver again.'

Helen's mind was racing. Oliver had stayed in the cottage just so that he could be with her? 'That doesn't mean he loves me. That just means he's kind. As you say, ''Pure Oliver.'' He would have done the same thing for anyone.'

'You need more evidence?' Tom thrust his hands in his pocket. 'In order to create a job for you, he bought his practice nurse a flight to Australia so that she could afford to visit her daughter.'

Helen shook her head. 'But she'd wanted to go for ages.'

'But she couldn't afford it,' Tom said gently. 'Oliver paid for the ticket and gave you the job because he decided that you needed the distraction of working to get you out of bed in the morning. He was afraid that if he left you on your own all day, you'd brood.'

Suddenly Helen remembered Hilda's surprise at hearing that Maggie had decided to go to Australia at such short notice.

'He didn't need a practice nurse?'

'Maggie is a perfectly good practice nurse.'

Helen swallowed in disbelief as she assimilated the enormity of the gesture. 'He did that for me?'

Tom nodded. 'He loves you, Helen. Enough to let you go because he thinks you love David.'

Helen stared at the train as it slowed and then turned her eyes back to Tom. 'He loves me?'

'And you love him.' Tom picked up her bags. 'So I suggest you cash in that ticket you bought and let me drop you back in the village. Last time I saw him he was dragging on his walking gear. It's what he always does when something stresses him. He takes to the hills.'

Helen was digesting everything that he'd said.

Had Oliver really thought she was going back to David?

Had he thought that he was making the decision easier for her?

She stood for a minute and then gave Tom a smile. 'Do you know where he's gone?'

'I've got a good idea.'

Helen breathed a sigh of relief. 'In that case, do you think you can drop me at the cottage so that I can borrow Bryony's walking clothes one more time? And then I need you to point me in the right direction.'

She found Oliver by the lake, at a place they'd walked to together several times over the past month.

He was sitting on a rock, throwing stones into the

water. He stood up as she approached, his expression neutral.

'You shouldn't walk in the mountains by yourself—you might get lost.'

Helen shrugged. 'I was careful. You see, I have this friend who taught me a game.'

The wind played with his dark hair. 'And what game is that?'

'You memorise different landmarks on the way.' Helen turned to look back down the path she'd taken. 'I passed a boulder shaped like a sheep, a patch of ice shaped like Africa. If I had to find my way back without getting lost, I could.'

He was silent for a moment, a muscle working in his lean jaw. When he finally spoke his voice was slightly hoarse. 'What are you doing here, Helen?'

'Looking for you.' She closed her eyes and breathed in the air. 'It's lovely here.'

'Helen…'

He looked so remote, so unlike Oliver, that for a moment her courage faltered. And then she remembered everything that Tom had told her and that gave her the strength she needed.

'Actually, I'm here because I need to ask you a question. If I ask you a question, will you give me an honest answer, Oliver?'

His expression was wary. 'That depends on the question.'

As a response it was less than encouraging, but she ploughed on anyway. This time she wasn't going to give up until she'd told him how she felt.

'Do you love me, Oliver?'

He flinched as though she'd struck him and

dragged his eyes away from hers, staring out across the mountains. 'What sort of a question is that?'

'An important one.' Suddenly her hands were shaking and she had butterflies in her stomach, but still she carried on, trying not to be put off by the fact that his hands were thrust firmly in his pockets. 'Last night you told me you loved me. I want to know if you meant it, or if it was something you say to every woman you make love to.'

He didn't move and he didn't look at her. 'I don't say it to every woman.'

'So, is that a yes?'

His hard jaw tensed and for a moment she thought he wasn't going to answer.

Then he stirred. 'Yes. I love you. Now what?'

Her heart lifted but he still didn't turn to face her so she walked around until she was in front of him.

'Now you can ask me a question.'

Finally his eyes met hers. 'Helen, I—'

'I expect you want to ask me about David,' she said quietly, 'so I'll just tell you anyway. I don't love David, Oliver. I'm not going with David. In fact, I should probably tell you that I intend to settle down in the Lake District with my family.'

Oliver was silent for a long moment, his blue eyes fixed on hers, his expression unreadable. Then he cleared his throat. 'Your family?'

'That's right.' She was taking a huge risk but she'd decided that it was worth it. 'For a while there's just going to be me and the man I love, but pretty soon I'm sure we'll have babies because I'm dying to be a mother and he's going to be a great dad. And if we're going to have lots of children we need to make a start.'

There was a long, pulsing silence and Oliver finally stirred. 'This man you love…'

'Yes?'

'He doesn't live in London?'

She gave a smile. 'He'd hate living in London. The man I love was born to live in the mountains. They're part of who he is.'

'Sounds a pretty weird choice of partner to me.' Oliver's voice was hoarse and he still hadn't touched her. 'Why would a London girl like you love a man like that?'

'You want to know what I love about him?' Helen's voice was soft. 'I love the fact that he cares so much about everyone. I love the fact he cares enough to see patients on his day off and pretend his roof needs fixing just so that he can keep an eye on a friend of his sister's that he doesn't even know.'

Oliver sucked in a breath. 'Helen—'

'I love the way he laughs all the time and I love the way he kisses.' Helen paused, digging her nails into her palms. 'And I love the way he pretends that he doesn't love me so that I can leave without feeling guilty.'

Oliver's eyes locked on hers. 'But you don't want to leave?'

She shook her head. 'Never again.' She huddled deeper inside her coat and stamped her feet to keep warm. *Surely he'd touch her soon?* 'My home is here. With you. If you want me, that is.'

And finally the tension seemed to drain out of him.

He gave a groan and dragged her into his arms, his voice muffled as he buried his face in her neck. 'Oh, God, Helen, I thought I'd lost you. When I saw you with David I thought I'd lost you.' He squeezed her tightly and then pushed her away slightly so that he could look at her. 'Once I heard you say you were glad he'd come, I thought that was it.'

'When you walked out, I almost died.' Helen put her arms around his neck, sliding her fingers into his hair, loving the way it felt. 'I couldn't get rid of David fast enough. But then I came to the surgery and you were so cold…'

'It was the only way I could stop myself from breaking down and begging you to stay,' he confessed in a raw tone, 'and I didn't want to do that to you. I wanted you to make the decision yourself, without pressure from me. I thought you'd already made that decision.'

'I'd already sent David away when I found you at the practice. I came to tell you that I loved you,' Helen told him, oblivious to the biting wind which buffeted both of them. 'But after you told me that last night was a mistake, there didn't seem much point.'

Oliver groaned and cupped her face in his hands. 'Last night wasn't a mistake, angel.' He lowered his mouth to hers, his kiss so hot and full of promise that she felt her body shiver. Only when both of them were struggling for breath did he lift his head. 'Last night was the single most perfect thing that has ever happened to me. When I woke up this morning and you were already downstairs, I assumed I'd frightened you away by telling you that I loved you.'

'I think I frightened myself,' Helen admitted, colour rising in her cheeks. 'It was so… I mean, I never—'

'Neither did I.' Oliver kissed her again. 'And when I saw you with David…'

'I told him that I was glad he'd come, because I

thought there were things I wanted to know,' Helen said quietly. 'I wanted to know how he could have ended our relationship the way he did, without seeing me face to face. Then I saw him and realised that actually I didn't even care anymore. I didn't care why he did it that way. All I cared about was you.'

'You were in his arms.'

'He pulled me there. I left them very quickly,' Helen said and Oliver let out a long breath.

'He's rich, Helen.'

She glanced around her, breathing in the air and sighing with pleasure as she looked at the mountains. 'What's rich?' She turned back to him. 'Rich is being with the person you love.'

He cupped her face in his hands. 'I thought you didn't believe that love could happen quickly.'

'I've learned a lot of things in the past few weeks,' she said softly. 'Like the fact that I love mountains. And that I don't want to go back to London. And that love can happen in a breath and when you're least expecting it. I arrived here broken-hearted but you made me see that what I felt for David wasn't love. Love is what I feel for you.'

'And is it enough?' His voice was hoarse and he stroked a hand around her face and tilted her chin. 'Is it enough to make you leave behind the stilettos and the suits? Your big city life? Is it asking too much of you to make you live here?'

She smiled. 'I want to live here. I want to be here when Hilda moves into her new flat. I want to know how things go with Anna and her new boyfriend and—' her eyes twinkled '—I even want to know about Howard Marks's sex life.'

Oliver grinned. 'I can assure you, you don't!'

Helen laughed. 'Well, what I mean is, I want to be part of this great community. I know I can't carry on being your practice nurse, but I still want to be part of everything.'

'Ah.' Something flickered in Oliver's eyes. 'About the practice nurse job...'

Helen's gaze softened. 'I can't believe you paid for Maggie to visit her daughter just to create a job for me.'

Oliver rubbed a hand across the back of his neck. 'It seems my generous gesture has rather backfired.'

'How?'

Oliver gave a wry smile. 'Maggie called this morning to say that she's enjoying herself so much she'd like extended leave of absence. I need a new practice nurse.'

Helen's mouth fell open. 'Oh!'

'Yes—"oh."' He shook his head. 'I must admit I didn't have the best morning. First I saw you with David and then my practice nurse decides not to come back.'

Helen kissed him. 'But the day is improving,' she said softly, 'because I happen to know someone who would make a great practice nurse. If only in the short term.'

Oliver dragged his mouth away from hers reluctantly. 'Short term?' His voice was husky and his eyes were still on her lips. 'Why short term?'

She blushed slightly. 'Because we were both a little carried away last night, that family of ours may be arriving sooner rather than later.'

Oliver stared at her and then a huge smile spread across his face. 'I might have made you pregnant—'

'Stop sounding so smug. If you have, you'll soon be interviewing a new practice nurse.'

'I don't care.' Oliver gave a groan and kissed her gently. 'I hope I did make you pregnant. I want to have lots of babies. I probably should have told you that before.'

Her insides melted. 'If you're the father, I want lots of babies, too. I love you.'

'And I love you, too.' He glanced back along the path she'd taken. 'Can you remember the way home?'

'Of course. Boulder shaped like a sheep and ice like Africa. 'Why?'

His blue eyes gleamed wickedly. 'Because I don't think we should leave this baby thing to chance. We should go home and try again.'

She lifted her mouth to his. 'That, Dr Hunter, sounds like a very good idea.'

MILLS & BOON®   1204/03b

Live the emotion

Medical
romance™

THE DOCTOR'S TENDER SECRET *by Kate Hardy*

(London City General)

On the hectic paediatrics ward of London City General,
love just isn't running smoothly for Dr Brad Hutton and
Dr Zoe Kennedy. They may be instantly smitten with
each other once again, but the secrets they have kept
locked away make their future together uncertain. For
Brad, the solution lies in putting his past behind him.
But Zoe's secret goes a lot deeper…

AIRBORNE EMERGENCY *by Olivia Gates*

(Air Rescue)

Surgeon Cassandra St James couldn't wait to join the
Global Aid Organisation's flying Jet Hospital – until she
encountered mission leader Vidal Santiago. What was
this millionaire plastic surgeon – the man she loved and
loathed – doing on a humanitarian mission? Had she
misjudged him? And could she control the unwanted
passion that flared between them?

OUTBACK DOCTOR IN DANGER *by Emily Forbes*

When an explosion rocks a peaceful Outback town,
flying doctor Matt Zeller is on hand to help. He hasn't
been emotionally close to anyone for years, and has
dedicated himself to his work – then he meets Nurse
Steffi Harrison at the scene. She's due to stay in town
for just a few weeks – but after knowing her for mere
moments Matt knows he wants her to stay!

On sale 7th January 2005

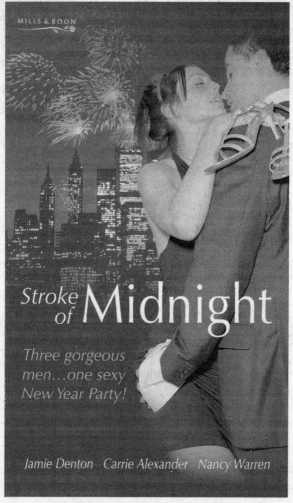

FREE!

4 Books
and a surprise gift!

We would like to take this opportunity to thank you for reading this Mills & Boon® book by offering you the chance to take FOUR more specially selected titles from the Medical Romance™ series absolutely FREE! We're also making this offer to introduce you to the benefits of the Reader Service™—

- ★ **FREE home delivery**
- ★ **FREE gifts and competitions**
- ★ **FREE monthly Newsletter**
- ★ **Exclusive Reader Service offers**
- ★ **Books available before they're in the shops**

Accepting these FREE books and gift places you under no obligation to buy, you may cancel at any time, even after receiving your free shipment. Simply complete your details below and return the entire page to the address below. You don't even need a stamp!

YES! Please send me 4 free Medical Romance books and a surprise gift. I understand that unless you hear from me, I will receive 6 superb new titles every month for just £2.69 each, postage and packing free. I am under no obligation to purchase any books and may cancel my subscription at any time. The free books and gift will be mine to keep in any case.

M4ZEF

Ms/Mrs/Miss/Mr ....Initials...

BLOCK CAPITALS PLEASE

Surname ....

Address...

....

....Postcode.......................................

Send this whole page to:
UK: FREEPOST CN81, Croydon, CR9 3WZ